T0207963

Eternal Eye

Eternal Eye

AI M Scott

ETERNAL EYE

iUniverse books may be ordered through booksellers or by contacting:

*iUniverse
1663 Liberty Drive
Bloomington, IN 47403
www.iuniverse.com
1-800-Authors (1-800-288-4677)*

*ISBN: 978-1-4917-5156-5 (sc)
ISBN: 978-1-4917-5157-2 (e)*

Library of Congress Control Number: 2014919001

Print information available on the last page.

iUniverse rev. date: 3/02/2015

1

Balad, Iraq-2003

Major David Allan hugged the dry ground tightly as whistling bullets pierced the moonless night sky above his head. Pinging sounds from 7.62 mm rounds clinked off the armored vehicles next to him. Rolling his Kevlar Helmet covered head slightly to one side, he could make out Captain Moran lying in the darkness next to him. He was motionless and his eyes gazed back at David with haunting emptiness. Moran's mouth was open; blood draining onto the parched farmland just outside the base camp in Iraq. David stared back at Moran, just moments ago, so full of vigor and life.

"Phil! Phil!" Major Allan yelled, realizing the stark reality but not wanting to believe it. The returning fire from the 4th Infantry Division's arsenal of the M249 guns mounted on the Humvees caused his ears to ring like a high-pitch siren.

Other soldiers, spread across the field, unloaded return fire from their individual M-16's. Gunfire was deafening; muzzle flashes lit up the blackness. Somewhere down range the barrage of ammo sought out the source from the AK- 47 s that suddenly stopped plinking off the Humvee's armor. The acrid smell of gunpowder permeated the darkness.

In his twenty-third year as an Army veteran, David thought for sure his 'Hooah' days were over. His assignment as a contracting officer was not a "kick-in-the-door" type of duty. Rather, as a Contingency Contracting Officer, he made sure the frontline troops had supplies, services, and armor protection they desperately needed.

Captain Phillip Moran, the HHC Company Commander from the 3rd Battalion, 4th Infantry Division (4ID) was a frequent customer who zealously looked after his soldiers and their needs. Major David Allan identified closely with the enlisted soldiers from Moran's unit, having been enlisted himself for seven years. He knew he could make a huge difference in providing the soldiers their ticket home and arriving in one piece.

"Hey sir, when are you going to come outside the wire with me and my boys so you can see what the real war is like?" Moran had asked him one day at the office.

"I don't know, maybe one of these nights, I suppose." David answered quickly and returned to administering another contract.

"Aw, come on sir, I won't let anything happen to you. I'll even sign you out an M-16 just in case." With CPT Moran's persistence and assurance of safety, David had finally been coerced into joining him on the night of December 13, 2003.

The shooting and yelling stopped. A distant voice yelled, "All's clear, sir. We got two of 'em!"

A young soldier, Moran's driver knelt beside the motionless captain. "Medic! Medic!"

He was yelling hysterically. "Oh God, sir, oh God!"

"He's gone," David said, matter-of-factly, and with a tinge of sadness in his voice.

"No, no, he can't be!"

Several soldiers rushed to the scene, the medic, dropping hard next to Moran. David knew that any attempt to save Moran's life was futile. The rest of the troops, ever vigilant, continued to scope the landscape with their weapons ready.

Each soldier was equipped with his own Night Observation Devices (NODs), goggles that were attached to the front of their helmets and designed to easily pull down over a warrior's eyes for instant night vision. David flipped his Nods down and looked out into the darkness. The silhouette of each appeared alien-like with an eerie green glow leaking out around their eyes from the protruding black scope. There was no illumination as the moon would not rise for a few more hours. But since the American GI was fitted with state of the art night vision, he could maneuver across the Iraqi battlefield as if it were day.

The Platoon Sergeant, SFC Rucker, stopped next to the medic. He looked up at him and shook his head slowly.

"Let's go! Keep your focus! There may be more!"

David watched the slow-moving squad inch their way forward through the patches of grass. The troops stopped suddenly and formed a circle around an area next to a dirt hill.

David got up and joined the group of warriors.

Flipping his nods up, he immediately noticed a small white pick-up truck parked by some date palm trees.

Sitting in the bed of the truck was a makeshift metal tube mounted on a steel plate. On the ground next to the rear left tire were two-miniature football shaped pieces of metal with fins attached at the end. "Mortar rounds," David uttered.

"Sir, are you alright?" SFC Rucker asked him.

"Physically, yes." David answered.

"Take a look at this, sir."

David sauntered over to the two bodies spaced apart by 20 meters or so and each still surrounded by a group of soldiers standing over them. Walking up to one of the bodies, he stared at the gruesome sight for a brief moment. Then he continued over to the other one who was at least recognizable. He remained silent.

This Iraqi didn't look any older than twenty. The lad had fallen victim to a few well aimed 5.56 rounds from an M-16. He couldn't distinguish the other's age, who had been shredded by a burst from the M249 gun.

The dead wore dirty tan shirts, black trousers, and beat up sandals on their feet. Lying next to each were their worn AK-47 assault rifles.

The young distinguishable one stared widely and lifelessly into the starry night sky with his mouth open as if he was in the midst of shouting in hopeful desperation, "Allah Akbar." A red disheveled scarf lay partially on his head. This macabre scene included puddles of blood oozing from the bodies and soaking into the dried mud mixed with sand.

David was angry.

"Senseless." He mumbled.

"Sir?" SFC Rucker responded.

"Captain Moran's death! It was a senseless tragedy!"

"Yes sir."

David walked away and reached into his pocket. Pulling out a smooth crystal marble, he held it up into the starry sky to see if the emerald-color swirl inside was still visible. *Maybe there's something in this thing to bring Phillip back magically,* he thought. It was still shining. It had not stopped shining since the time it was given to him by a female private in Kuwait.

Three months prior, David waited in a long line to use the phone while staying at Camp Wolf before his arrival to Balad. While sitting on a wooden bench, a soldier, who also happened to be a pretty young lady with sandy-colored hair escaping from beneath her desert boonie cap, sauntered over and sat next to him. He watched her sit and noticed her reaction when she discovered that next to her was a Major. "Oh, sorry sir, was somebody sitting here?"

"No, you're fine."

There was a moment of silence. David could tell she was conspicuously trying to see the various patches on his uniform. "Sir, can I ask you something?"

"Sure."

"Do you ever get use to this?"

The female soldier looked too young to be mixed up in this mess. David guessed she was about the same age as his own daughter, about nineteen or twenty. "What, you mean war?"

"Yes sir."

"Never get used to war if you can help it. You'll notice the longer you're in, the more we feel the need to be in everybody's business around the world."

David could see the puzzled look on the young private's face as if she wanted to simply burst out with a *HUH*? To her credit, she answered, "I'm not sure what you mean sir."

"That's okay, I'm not sure either." They both laughed.

"Don't get used to it, Private Gabriel." He continued while eyeing her nametag. "Never get used to it."

"How do you cope, I mean, measure your time, especially in such a wasteland?"

David thought the question to be interesting enough. "Funny you should ask." Thinking how he would answer her without seeming like a nut, he broached the subject thoughtfully. "I bought a few bags of marbles at Toys-R-us before leaving home and counted out 365 of them. Then, I bagged them up, brought them with me, and from day one, no matter where I was, I flicked one of them out into the night sky. This signified a day gone by."

"That's cool, sir!"

"I even found a glass vase at a market in Saudi that was able to contain most all of the marbles so I could watch the stack get lower, ever so slowly. Eventually, I filled the vase with the remaining ones that didn't initially fit. I should have taken a before-after picture in the beginning."

"How many years do you have in, if you don't mind me asking?"

"Not at all. I'm in my 23rd year, if you count the two years I did ROTC between my enlisted and officer time."

"Wow, that's a long time. I don't think that I could make it that long."

"It's been a good journey overall. There were a couple of things I would have changed."

"Like what, sir?"

"Well, if I had the crystal ball and could forecast events, I would have taken measures to stop the Oklahoma City bombing for one."

"How could you have done that?"

"Oh, I don't know, just saying. I would definitely have prevented the 9/11 events from happening. We wouldn't be here today, most likely."

"We all would have liked for that day never to happen."

The girl smiled and reached into her pocket, pulled out something tiny and held it towards David. "Have you ever seen anything like this before?"

David let it drop into his hand and saw a unique marble with a shining emerald swirl inside. To his astonishment, the swirl was in motion. Holding the marble up to one of the portable street lights for closer inspection, he was mesmerized by the immense beauty and color. "This is amazing! Where did you get this?"

"I came across it at home."

"Oh? Where's home?" He was still staring into the marble.

The girl smiled. "I need to go now, sir. That one is yours; keep it please. I have more."

David held the marble out towards the young private. "I couldn't possibly take this from you without compensating you in some way."

She stood to go without extending her hand. "Sir, it's been a pleasure. My name is Michel. I need to run. Good luck in Balad." She did not take the marble.

The young girl disappeared into the crowd of soldiers while David sat dumbfounded. *Did I mention anything about going to Balad?* He wondered.

While David contemplated the unfolding events in front of him, several miles to the north under the same moonless night approximately 600 soldiers from the same 4th Infantry Division were in the process of conducting a raid in the small town of Ad Dawr. A power outage, not uncommon, kept the whole area in darkness. Based on reliable and recent intelligence, the 4th ID soldiers, accompanied by Special Forces specializing in hunting down "High Valued Targets" (HVT's), swept quickly through a farm compound near the banks of the Tigris River.

Bursting into a two-room hut inside a mud-walled area, they found two beds, strewn with clothing and a kitchen containing cans of spam, and boxes of rotting oranges. Outside, between two farmhouses surrounded by sheep pens, an old, worn-out rug covered in dirt laid flat on the ground. One of the soldiers called for backup and after knocking the dirt off the rug slowly pulled it back revealing a thick piece of Styrofoam. Beneath the Styrofoam appeared to be a small hole.

Sounds could be heard in the hole. "Someone's in here!" the soldier yelled. Yanking a grenade off of his vest he was about to drop it "down the hatch." Suddenly, uplifted hands appeared, one of them holding a pistol.

Kicking the weapon away from the hand they quickly seized the man beginning to crawl out of the hole and yanked him the remaining way out. The soldiers stared in disbelief. What they saw was a beleaguered old man with a scraggly gray and white beard.

"I am Saddam Hussein. I am the President of Iraq. I want to negotiate." The man said in English.

Standing there dumbfounded one of the soldiers replied, "President Bush sends his regards."

2

A week after David's mission with CPT Moran ended, he found himself waiting; again. Sitting casually on the splintered bench, legs stretched out in front of him, his suede desert boots resting on the loosely, gravel covered dusty ground, he observed the wooden benches, which formed irregular lines beneath the makeshift tin rooftop, held in place by several wooden beams. Like the soldiers around him, male, female, young, old, sergeants, lieutenants, and even a few civilians, he waited. Everyone waited for the flight status, whether or not they could leave this God-forsaken country on this particular night and return home for a two-week vacation. David looked forward to his time in Orlando, Florida, hoping to arrive before Christmas.

It was 1441 by his watch when an Air Force Tech Sergeant came out without a hat, clipboard in his hand and sporting the latest style of Oakley sunglasses. He sported the same tan colored desert camouflage uniform as most everyone else sitting around.

After listening to him make a brief announcement, David pulled out a folded greeting card from his carry-on bag, trying to keep it clean.

My darling girl, when God created you, he had you distinctly in mind; adding a brilliant shade of green to your eyes that glowed like emeralds; a ray of sunlight emitting from your face whenever you parted your lips and displayed your sparkling smile; your heart of gold, warmed by the fires from heaven. He also thought of me; how could he not have? He waited for the perfect time, three years beyond your birth, before deciding to form my existence; a life designed to become the man for you, one who would love you with all of his heart and soul until the day he died.

He originally wrote those words to his wife, Sherry, while he was deployed in 1991 to Saudi Arabia during Desert Storm. She had placed it in his Bible before he departed for Iraq.

David's thoughts were snapped by an Air Force sergeant yelling above the background noise of aircraft. "All right, can I have your attention please? The flight has been delayed due to mechanical upgrades. You can be released from the area but please be back by 1800. We will conduct a manifest roll call at that time."

David grabbed his rucksack, slung it over his shoulder and looked for a way back to the office. *Why waste time*, he thought, *with all of the procurements and business taking place.* The rest of his gear, a large duffle bag, was already secured onto a pallet along with everybody else's gear. He could hear the moans and groans mixed with the curses from the crowd as he headed for the intersection just outside the terminal to catch a ride to his office, which was a juxtaposition of trailers fastened together.

When David had arrived to Balad four months before his allotted time off for Christmas Leave, he came straight from a tour in Saudi Arabia. It was in the middle of the day, just before lunch. At 100 degrees Fahrenheit, the weather was slowly beginning to change from the 130 degree summer. His travel originated from Riyadh and passed through Kuwait City with a stop for a few days at Camp Arifjan, one of the new American enclaves. Then, he was driven to camp Wolf to catch the flight into Iraq.

Remembering his first taste of Iraq, the blast of heat was his first welcome once the rear door of the aircraft opened like a mouth to a hydraulic drone and high pitch. The blast of arid furnace hurried inside to spread its overly warm welcome to the waiting soldiers, still strapped in the canvass seats.

Everyone waited in the blazing oven while all of the equipment and gear was loaded from the plane first. An Air Force Tech Sergeant entering the plane shouted, "Follow me, please and remove your headgear before leaving the aircraft!"

Then the passengers grabbed their bags and one by one, filed down the ramp onto the tarmac. With sweat already pouring down the side of his face, David joined the line, one by one, down the ramp and onto the tarmac. Major Allan, dressed in his Desert Combat Uniform (DCUs), sported a stylish pair of Oakley sunglasses, purchased while in Riyadh, realizing that there was no uniformed or standard issue when it came to eyewear. The line of troops followed the Air Force tech Sergeant across the hot tarmac, amidst numerous C-130's, C-5 Galaxy's, and Blackhawk helicopters. The overpowering smell of diesel and other variety of fumes filled the air. As they moved along, an Air Force Sergeant was leading another line of soldiers, mingled with a few civilians towards the aircraft that David and his fellow soldiers had just departed.

"Welcome to 'Mortaritasville," someone yelled from the line above the sounds of aircraft engines and flapping rotors.

Major Allan would later discover first hand why Anaconda earned its nickname, along with the unflattering name, "Bombaconda." Random mortars and rockets would frequently land somewhere on the compound, often causing chaos and temporarily halting operations.

David followed the line, occasionally feeling the marble that was given to him just before the trip, and rolled it around in his palm.

Now, four months later, David was more than ready to go home for some Christmas R&R. He had spent the previous five months in Saudi Arabia, training for his new job as a Contingency Contracting Officer, and then was transferred to LSA Anaconda to support the Combined Joint Task Force-7 operations, consisting of more than 20,000 coalition forces. It was up to him, and others like him, to establish trusting business relations and a vendor base among the local Iraqi's to procure the necessary supplies and services for the soldiers and their mission.

David knew that things wouldn't be the same when he returned home for the holidays, he was sure of that. His dog, "Rusky" died two months after David deployed to the war zone. David still remembered Rusky's look of bewilderment when the dog stood on his hind two legs peering out the front window as David departed. David imagined then that Rusky was probably thinking, *Will I ever see you again?*

Only in paradise now, my friend, David thought.

His daughter, Jenny, had just graduated from high school and his son, Robert, was nearing the completion of his third year at the West Point Academy in New York. David pondered these things and couldn't wait to get back home to the "perfect" vacation to see his family. He couldn't even define what "perfect" would be, but just knew that it had to be perfect!

The manifest process ensued again at 1800. Three hours later, a different Air Force representative appeared and announced, "I'm sorry everyone, but this scheduled flight has been delayed until tomorrow morning."

The groans and curses could be heard even louder than before when given the same news earlier in the day. An agitated Army Lieutenant Colonel walked up to the Air Force Sergeant and demanded to speak with his OIC. "Sir, I know it sucks, but we'll make sure that you are on your flight first thing in the morning."

The officer wouldn't budge. "Okay, sir, follow me, please."

David did not want to wait around so he found a ride, once again, this time back to his leaky trailer where he resided so he could get another night of sleep, joining his tiny roommates, "Mickey" and "Minnie," the two local rats.

The following day, all of the same processes was repeated, including the frequent delays. Finally, around 2000, the final manifest was called out and the line of soldiers, marines, airmen, and civilians walked towards the large silhouette of the C-5 Galaxy jet aircraft. The C-5 was the largest in the fleet and could carry M-1 Abram tanks in the main body while the troops slept upstairs in a passenger compartment. David remembered the last time he was on one of these as he was headed to Saudi Arabia during Desert Storm 12 years before.

The line moved towards the aircraft and then stopped suddenly, causing some to bump into the ones in front of them. The Lieutenant Colonel was amongst the soldiers. The wait began again and the rumor spreading up and down the line was that the aircraft was experiencing more mechanical difficulty. The colonel was about to go ballistic with this news. Major Allan joined most of those in line and removed his rucksack from his back, plopped it on the tarmac, and leaned against it, his legs stretched out in front of him. Small chatter was exchanged but nothing worth remembering, except for the humorous observation of the Lieutenant Colonel's animated antics and profound speech.

David looked into the night sky to catch a glimpse of the sparkling lights overhead. Locating the Big Dipper was always his first choice and then he oriented himself from there by tracing its lead to the North Star. Often, he scanned the expanse to search for a shooting star. There were none on this night that he could see. Reaching into his pocket, David pulled out the smooth marble and held it up to the sky. The emerald swirl inside seemed to be moving with more intensity for whatever reason, David could not figure out.

In the crowd of air force technicians milling about the aircraft, one of them lifted his hand in the air, circled his fist with his index finger pointing skyward, and yelled, "Let's roll. Wheels up!"

Everyone cheered, then quickly grabbed their bags and moved forward like a caterpillar into the large mouth of the bird. David pocketed his marble and stood up with the rest. Then they inched forward, once again, moving to the big jumbo jet silhouetted on the dark tarmac in front of them.

Bright lights, shining everywhere, greeted their entrance into the aircraft. The line continued along to the rear of the aircraft and up the metal steps to the second floor. The first few passengers lunged for an empty seat before the seats were taken. Next, the aisle seats quickly filled.

Major Allan was able to get a seat on the right side of the aircraft, next to where a window would be in a passenger jet. A female lieutenant sat down next to him. They exchanged a couple of one-liners about finally being able to finally go home. Everyone got settled and maneuvered their gear where possible; strapped themselves in and listened to any instructions provided while waiting for takeoff.

Thirty minutes later, the C-5 was slowly moving into position at the end of the tarmac. After further delays, David could hear the high, winding pitch of the jet engines being revved to a thunderous roar and then the jet lurching forward. He remembered this distinctive sound from when he and Sherry were first married and lived in a small trailer, just outside Pope Air Force base. Although not the only cause, but anytime the C-5 roared into action, their trailer shook and rocked.

The interior was now dark, the passengers quiet. David felt the rapid, increasing thrust of speed through his body and then felt the liftoff. *"This pilot must be afraid of ground fire,"* David thought to himself, as the jet shot into a steep incline, reminding him of what it might be like inside a rocket. Not that he was ever in one, except for the "Mars" ride at Epcot. He began silently whispering, "Straighten up, level out. Hurry!"

After several minutes, the C-5 began to level. David leaned back and closed his eyes, thanking God that he was finally airborne, and on his way home to see his family. He especially looked forward to seeing his wife, Sherry, the girl he loved and had been married to for nearly 22 years.

At some point, his drifting thoughts faded into sleep. His dreams, sweet at first, abruptly turned violent and he found himself back in the capital of Colombia during a terrorist attack. Something like a bomb exploded and David's head snapped forward, causing him to open his eyes in fright. Rapidly blinking and adjusting to the darkness, David looked around. None of the other passengers in sight were sleeping, but rather dozily looking around like he was.

Suddenly, the jet dropped straight down, causing a loud thud-type sound as if it landed on something and bounced back up. "Jesus!" somebody yelled.

The lieutenant next to David looked worried as she clutched the seat in front of her and looked for an air bag. The plane took another bounce, much like the first one, only worse. The bouncing seemed to be getting harder.

"What the hell is going on?" The Lieutenant Colonel was yelling and preparing to remove himself from his seat. This turned out not to be a wise decision.

The jet jerked again, sending the Lieutenant Colonel down the aisle and against the wall with a thud. He hit hard. Nobody could assist him because the plane began bouncing up and down even more and shaking like one of those overpriced simulated rides at a theme park.

The plane tilted to its side violently, sending passengers grasping for something solid. Equipment was flying around. The lieutenant next to David screamed. David tried to look at her but he was busy blocking a flying rucksack from striking him in the head. David's head started to uncontrollably rock back and forth with the force of the aircraft, now spinning to its left and then to its right.

The fact that the C-5 was not in a "nose-dive" presented a glimmer of hope for David. "Dear God, help us through this! Get us through! Please G…."

The lights flickered on briefly and then back off. There were popping sounds, like firecrackers.

The yelling and commotion increased and reached a fever pitch when the huge aircraft bounced again. This time, the impact was all she could take. David was spinning around like a top, still strapped to his seat. He held on for dear life. Rucksacks, weapons, and other equipment flew past his head like missiles. He still held on the best he could.

For a brief second, there was a glimpse of the Lieutenant Colonel flying past David like a large sack. He was limp. Seats flew by, metal ripped, and the sky opened before David's eyes. David's seat suddenly lifted up and was sucked out of the jet as if a tornado in Kansas had grabbed it and flung it like a toy. David remained intact in his seat.

While David was spinning in the air, a leg flew past him and something like water splashed across his face. There was also the jagged piece of the fuselage turning along the side of him, and he hoped that there would be no contact. Sailing at full speed, his back into the wind, and still strapped to his seat, David could see what was left of the aircraft as it sat on the desert floor in several pieces. Patches of fire spread across the sand like miniature bonfires.

David wondered how bad it would hurt when he finally landed on the ground. The desert floor rushed up towards him. He drew a deep breath and then yelled, "I love you Sherry!"

"Aaaahhhh!" David felt the jarring sensation of impact while remaining attached to his seat. The force of impact kicked up a pile of sand that fell back down on him like rain.

His body ripped from the cushions as both he and the seat, now in separate parts, bounced and rolled across the wasteland. The bouncing stopped. David opened his eyes, then spit. He could not move his 175 pound frame, but he wiggled his fingers. A third of his face was buried in the sand but his nose was above the surface, clearing his nostrils to rapidly grasp oxygen. "I'm still alive!" He choked. "Oh God, I hurt. Everywhere."

Surrounded by darkness David heard the crackling sound of fire echoing near him and for a couple of seconds, a male voice yelled, "Help me, help me!" But that sound soon faded away until everything was quiet. The landscape seemed misty and dark. For several minutes there was only silence. In the distance, David thought that he heard the sound of rotor blades beating against the night sky. Then a gust of wind blowing in increments whipped across his motionless body. *Could it be the sound of angel wings swooping to pick me up and take me home?* David thought.

"Sherry," he whispered. The stars above him twinkled brightly, and then faded, then blinked again, as if they were sending a coded message from heaven. David felt weaker and weaker. A sparkling emerald light emitted from the sand, just out of David's reach. His mind reached for it but his hand didn't move; not even an inch. A numb sensation engulfed his body, and then he closed his eyes.

3

David's eyes fluttered a few seconds before he completely opened his eyes. Slowly adjusting his focus, he made out a dim blurry figure standing over him. *Was it an angel? Was it Jesus?* The soft hand of a woman was holding his. A voice spoke softly, "David! David! Can you hear me?"

"Yes," he managed. The figure became slightly more distinguishable now. Sherry?"

Leaning closer to him, until her face brushed his, she said, "Oh my God, Yes, darling, it is me, your wife!"

David felt her soft lips on his face mixed with drops of water, one of which rolled down his cheek into the side of his mouth. He could taste the saltiness of her teardrops as he licked his lips.

"Oh my God, David, I love you, I love you, so much!" Sherry looked around the room for a nurse, an orderly, a doctor, anybody!

One of the medical technicians hurried into the room after noticing the activity on the monitor screen at her desk. She jumped up to retrieve the doctor after witnessing Major Allan wake up and held his wife's hand.

Sherry lifted her head and stared affectionately into his eyes. What a beautiful sight to behold. David smiled, and then he laughed, a laugh of pure joy and pleasure. Why not, he just survived a horrific plane crash somewhere in the Iraqi desert, and here he was waking up to the most beautiful woman he had ever laid eyes on.

"Am I dreaming? Is this heaven?"

"No honey, you are back home, you are here, in the USA!"

Sherry leaned forward to give him another kiss when a military Doctor entered the room with a uniformed nurse tagging closely behind.

"Lieutenant Allan, can you hear me? I'm Dr. Meyers, your neurologist, and you are at the Walter Reed Army Medical Center.

David could see that he wore the rank of a Colonel on his collar.

"Yes sir, I can hear you," David answered, wondering why he was being addressed as a Lieutenant.

Dr. Meyers smiled, and then exchanged glances with Sherry and then continued.

"Lieutenant Allan, you suffered quite a traumatizing head injury and have been in a coma for three months. Do you recollect anything at all, anything that happened to you in Kuwait?"

The Medical assistant returned to the room and started chattering with the nurse.

Sherry could see that David looked puzzled. "Umm, sort of. Wasn't I in a C-5 jet that crashed or was shot down shortly after taking off from Balad?"

Dr. Meyers smiled politely, "I tell you what, why don't you get some rest for now and we can discuss everything later, okay?"

Dr. Meyers quickly turned to Sherry and with a slight nod, led her to the front door. "I'll be right back honey; I just want to speak with the Doctor for a moment. I promise that I won't leave you and will be right here."

"Sure thing," David answered, his hand slowly reaching for his head as if to feel for its existence. Then he tried to piece together the actual events. There was a slight throbbing pain in his head but nothing severe.

"Hello Lieutenant Allan, I'm Major Calloway, and I'm just going to take your vitals for now, okay?"

"Okay Major. By the way, why does everybody keep calling me 'Lieutenant?'

The nurse glanced at him momentarily but refrained from answering his question. "Just remember that you went through a severe accident and are in the process of recovering. I believe that when I finish taking your vital signs, everything will indicate that you are on the mend and will be able to return to your home at Ft. Bragg sooner than you know it."

Fort Bragg? I haven't been at Fort Bragg since 1994.

David thought hard, holding his hand to his head again. It was still there. The doctor told Sherry that David had suffered a moderate case of intracranial injury and because a team of medics were quickly on the scene within the first 30 minutes, his chances were very good that he would wake up from his coma and be able to live a full normal life.

"Thank God it is still there," David said as he felt the cuff on his right arm squeeze tighter and tighter.

"What is?" Nurse Calloway asked.

"My noggin!"

She chuckled briefly. "Of course it is."

"Fort Bragg?" He thought again. "I haven't been there since the mid-nineties."

"Let's get you to sit up a bit," Nurse Calloway said, her eyes shifting briefly towards him. The more you move around, the better." She began taking his vital signs by placing a Blood Pressure cuff around his right bicep. After listening through a stethoscope, she removed the BP cuff, and turned back to David with a cheerful smile and a wink. "You will be just fine. I'll let the Doctor know that you are 'normal."

David could see that Major Calloway stopped and spoke with Doctor Meyers. Sherry returned to his side, clutching his hand. She looked as vibrant as ever and she smiled her beautiful smile, grabbing David's hand tightly. Doctor Meyers told me that you could be coming home soon, but that he will need to run some more tests."

"How long have I been here? Will you stay with me?" David pleaded.

"Of course I will, from the moment you were brought here until we return home. The kids will be sooo happy to see their daddy back home in Fayetteville and well."

"Fayetteville? Daddy? Honey, aren't the kids a bit old for, 'daddy?" Then, before he could go on with more questions and Sherry had time to respond to his bizarre behavior, and maybe because his eyes were becoming more focused with time, he suddenly realized that Sherry looked 12 years younger than when he had left her just seven months before. And her hair! He had not seen her with that color, style and length since he returned from Desert Storm in 1991.

Sherry looked into his eyes, "David, the Doctor said that you might have memory loss and that you may not be thinking coherently for a period of time. But, he expects a full recovery and everything will be back to normal in no time at all!"

David wondered. "Sherry, you look beautiful, I, I just can't remember ..." he was cut short by a young sergeant wearing whites wheeling in a cart of food. Major Calloway followed close behind.

"Here you are, sir," the Sergeant said; A gourmet meal of Jell-O, pudding, and soup extravaganza and your choice of selected beverages from the gallery!"

"Thanks, Sergeant," David managed.

Major Calloway watched as she jotted down some notes on the clipboard she was carrying. "Your system will need to become accustomed to solid food again. You had been drinking the choicest foods for the past two months."

Sherry helped him sit up and while doing so, managed to bump into the cart, sending a splattering of soup onto the bed. "Oh, I'm so sorry!"

The young sergeant rushed into the bathroom to grab some towels off the rack while Major Calloway and Sherry lifted the cover from David's bed in an attempt to keep the slimy liquid from soaking through to his skin.

"It's okay, babe!" David chuckled. "It's really okay."

In a matter of time, David had the mess cleaned around him and he began to eat. Before he placed a fifth bite into his mouth, he hesitated briefly.

"Sherry, can you bring me a mirror?"

David wanted to see the extent of damage that a plane crash would cause, besides putting him into a coma.

Sherry did not see any harm in giving him a mirror since he had recovered fully from the various contusions and abrasions spread across his face, chest, arms, and legs. In fact, the healing process was nearly complete for his two non-severe fractured legs, shoulder, and arm. The last thing Sherry, and everyone else, waited to discover was whether or not David would come out of a Coma after three months. All of the attending physicians had given her a light of hope and recommended a waiting period once the swelling around his brain returned to normal.

Sherry held a mirror to his face. "Here, you keep eating and I will hold this for you."

David kept eating until Sherry placed the mirror up to his face. Dropping the fork, David grabbed the mirror from Sherry's hand and held it closer to his face. Moving the mirror around for a variety of views from different angles he looked intently beneath his eyes. Then he moved it around some more.

Besides seeing that his face was much thinner than he had grown accustomed to over the past several years, the wrinkles and the dark circles under his eyes were gone! Sherry giggled at his reaction, like somebody who just discovered the use of a mirror. More precisely, it was a man rediscovering his youth!

"Sherry, oh my God, those guys are good. Not only did they fix whatever happened to me, but they made me look years younger…just like you!"

Sherry took the mirror from him. He watched her, impressed by how young she looked.

"Stop being silly. You have always looked young for your age."

"You have too, but even now…

"Finish eating some food. You need to put on a bit more weight."

When David was finished eating, Sherry began picking up and taking charge of the clean-up process.

"David, when you are ready, I will be happy to take care of your bath detail."

David smiled like a little boy in a candy store when he heard that.

"Do you have Major Calloway's permission?"

"I don't need anybody's permission for that, however, the Doctor did tell me that I could administer any type of comfort that you desire as long as I am here taking care of you."

"Any type of comfort?"

Sherry smiled, "any type short of strenuous activity. That will have to come later."

They both smiled.

David finished his meal and was enjoying Sherry's company. "Honey, could you put on CNN or something, I'd like to hear the latest news about Iraq."

"Sure, hold on a second."

"I helped catch Saddam, you know."

Sherry just looked at him and smiled. "Here, let me turn this on for you."

The images on the screen showed a lot of celebration taking place around the country and on military bases. "Did Iraq surrender after Saddam's capture in the past two months? Are we out of Iraq already?"

Sherry didn't answer him but kept moving with the clean-up.

"Wait, these soldiers are wearing the 'chocolate chip' uniform; they're showing old footage of the Desert Storm celebration! That explains everything. Can you change the channel to Fox news or something more recent?"

Sherry looked a bit confused. "Fox news?"

"I don't see any news about the current war in Iraq or Afghanistan."

Sherry stopped what she was doing and walked over to David. Then she sat down next to him, placing her hands on both of his.

"David, I don't know what you remember or exactly what happened, but we kicked Saddam's butt back into Iraq and you liberated Kuwait."

"Yes bu…"

"And then, I am very sorry to say this, but you and your driver, SSG Schmidt went into Kuwait City shortly after the main assault and he drove over a land mind left behind by the Iraqi forces. SSG Schmidt did not survive. You don't remember any of this, do you?"

David was stunned. "No! That can't be! That never happened! SSG Schmidt returned with me in '91 to a grand Homecoming!"

Now it was Sherry's turn to be stunned. "David, what are you talking about? Your whole unit came home just two months ago; SSG Schmidt was not amongst them. You had already been flown to Frankfurt and then here to Walter Reed."

"I think I'm losing my mind!" David sounded like he was panicking.

"I'm sorry honey, here, just lay here a minute, I'll call the nurse."

David grabbed her arm. "Wait, please." He loosened his grip. "I'm sorry."

"Oh David, you have no reason to be sorry."

"Let me ask you something straight. Robby and Jennifer, where are they?"

David was referring to his and Sherry's two children.

"They're okay. They're with my mom, and your mom. They are at the house in Fayetteville."

David thought for a moment. "What grade are they in now?"

Sherry felt like he was coming to his senses and was trying to recollect his memory.

"Robby is in 2nd grade and Jennifer in 1st."

David stared hard at Sherry. She looked beautiful, young, just like she did 12 years before. He slowly lay back, reclining fully against the soft pillow. "I remember now. Wow, I, I can't believe this is happening."

"What is happening, David? Tell me what?"

"Nothing bad, I don't think. Sherry, are there any recent magazines laying around the waiting area or something, *Time, Newsweek*, maybe?"

"I'll go look. David," she began, but placed her hand on his head. "Do you feel alright?"

"Yes, honey, I don't have any pain right now."

"That's not what I meant, but this is good, I'm sure."

He reached for her hand and held it to his cheek.

"Robby and Jennifer, when will I get to see them?"

Sherry seemed relieved. "You'll get to see them sooner than you think. They can even call you tonight!"

"That will be great!" David said.

Sherry got up to find some magazines at David's request. David looked around the room and back up at the television. He picked up the small remote that Sherry had placed on the small table sitting next to his bed. Then he flipped through the channels.

David scanned the television screen and was both fascinated and confused by the revealing signs. He was either going through a very real dream, or else, somehow had slipped back into the past, or, quite simply, died and gone to heaven. He discounted the last option because he grew up believing that he would be met by Jesus in paradise when he arrived in heaven, and Walter Reed was no paradise. He also envisioned the possibility of seeing his grandfather and other close relatives who had previously left the earth. As far as he knew, Sherry had not departed the earth.

Sherry walked back into the room. "I found the latest Time magazine in the waiting room."

David snatched it from her hand. The cover had a young girl, looking like she was in her late teens or early twenties holding another girl, about a year old, on her shoulders. The caption read, "The Gift of Love: Story of Miracles and Moral Dilemmas."

More astonishing to David was the date on the cover, "June 17, 1991!" He opened the first page to read the contents. One caught his eye immediately. "America's Postwar Mood: Making sure of the Storm."

Sherry could see the expression on David's face. "What's wrong, honey?"

"You said that this is the latest edition of Time?"

"Yes, I think so, why?" She took it back from him to look at the cover.

"No reason," David said as he began to realize that indeed, he could no longer deny that something very strange and unexplainable occurred. Details of the plane crash would not escape him, especially the pain he had felt, the screams he heard; the taste of sand in his mouth. Somehow he survived but could not rationalize his current condition. Maybe he was still in a coma, somewhere in limbo between life on earth and eternity in heaven. How much should he try to understand? How much explanation should he search? How much-

"Honey?" Sherry asked. "Can I get you anything else?"

David smiled, "I have you, babe! You're all I need right now."

4

Sherry felt like a large load of bricks had been lifted off of her shoulders. David had only been on the Neurology wing of the hospital for three weeks, arriving there from the ICU. She was well aware that the most important role she could play as a supportive wife was to be the best advocate for David's recovery by making sure that he received the best medical care possible. She also wanted to make sure that David would have total access to the rehabilitation programs he would need for the full process. The U.S. army had assured her that they were more than sufficient to provide this type of full support. "Thank you, God," she whispered.

For three long months, an eternity to her, she had been at her husband's side, holding his hand, talking to him, singing to him, cleaning him. Now, everything seemed like it was going to be alright. Well, almost everything. "David has been acting strange," she had confided to her mother. "He talks about events that haven't happened yet, like Robby going to West Point and our home in Orlando, in exquisite detail."

David wasn't sure how much to reveal because he wanted to be sure himself so he always added, "Maybe I was just dreaming," when sharing with his wife. Deep inside however, he felt sure that he had actually lived the events that he described and witnessed firsthand their home in Orlando and Robby's departure to West Point.

The process of David emerging from his coma began slowly, weeks before. His rehabilitation began while he was still in a coma, thanks primarily to the respiratory therapist and her instructions to Sherry on maintaining David's pulmonary hygiene. It would be important for Sherry to help keep David free from pulmonary problems such as pneumonia or atelectasis and to recognize the preliminary signs.

Although David opened his eyes during this time period, he would fall asleep almost immediately. This cycle continued, each time his eyes opening a little longer. Shortly afterwards, he began moving his arms and legs, little at first, but then with enough purpose to reach out. His head began to move from side to side as well but his speech was still mumbled.

Now, in just a couple more days, David would be able to join her in the plush Hilton Garden Inn hotel that the Army, along with an anonymous donor, put up for her during her stay outside the capitol. He could join her on the small balcony overlooking the surrounding DC landscape where she had taken in the mixture of the vast and busy landscape of Maryland. This was the state that David was born in, she reminded herself, hoping that he would soon see it again.

Often, during her 3-month stay, she felt the need to get on the metro and ride it to the Federal Triangle, Smithsonian, or the L'Enfant Plaza, and then walk around admiring the Cherry Blossoms during its Peak Bloom in late March and early April. In fact, she was there long enough to witness the changes from the visible florets to its extension, peduncle elongation, and the eventual puffy white appearance, just prior to beholding the moment of full beauty.

Only once did she ride the metro to the Arlington cemetery to witness the changing of the guard. She only glanced past the white stones, hoping with all of her heart that David would not be amongst them; at least not anytime soon. She would go back to the hospital, and sit beside David, holding his hand. Sherry waited and watched, day after day, for any sign of emergence from the coma that David was experiencing.

During the waiting time period, Dr. Meyers conferred often with Sherry, explaining to her about the medical prognosis on Traumatic Brain Injury (TBI) and temporary verses permanent comatose conditions. He explained to her that some people experience long term problems with memory, fatigue, concentration, dizziness and even anger that could always be present long after full recovery. "Even in the event that David recovers quickly, it could take years to fully understand the extent of his injuries."

Sherry remained hopeful. She bit her lip and held back the tears more than once during these sessions with Dr. Meyers. "I love him; Dr. Meyers; our children love him! They wouldn't know what to do without him," she once told him. "He is their hero! He is our hero, their daddy, my husband!" She could not hold back the tears after that revelation.

Dr. Meyers had an open door policy when it came to discussing David's condition at length with Sherry. He seemed to admire her tenacity and the way she appeared to control her emotions during a very stressful time. At first, she thought that the Colonel was enthralled by David's survival and great chances of full recovery. No doubt, this would have been a recognizable accomplishment if Major Allan had fully recovered from the injuries' he received. Dr. Meyers could write in medical journals about the breakthroughs on war time TBI's and receive numerous accolades.

It wasn't until Dr. Meyers began asking to see Sherry more frequently and proceeded to share things that she had already heard him say before, when she began to wonder if his interest extended beyond David's medical condition. "I'm probably just imagining his interest," she thought to herself.

Then, she received word from the hospital staff that the Army had made arrangements for her to move into the Hilton Garden from the Travel

Lodge in Silver Springs. Dr. Meyers even invited her to dine with him at the hotel restaurant when she "Bumped into him" while checking in to her new accommodations. Caught by surprise, and not wanting to seem rude, she accepted his invitation.

Not long into the dinner conversation the topic began to shift from David's condition and the medical breakthroughs, to more personal background matters. Although Sherry was somewhat naïve when it came to subversive propositions, she wisely caught on soon enough to avoid long, direct eye contact with him. She also consciously withdrew her hands naturally towards her drink whenever the Colonel appeared to moving closer in her direction.

Whether or not he had any subtle ideas about Sherry, it was obvious that Colonel Meyers enjoyed her presence. She was a pretty, green-eyed brunette, with shoulder-length thick hair who had beyond the call of duty type resolve. Colonel Meyer's feelings could have been influenced by the fact that his wife had left him years before when circumstances became harsh in their lives. He had even told Sherry that he admired her disposition and sense of loyalty that she displayed towards her husband, despite the odds of a full recovery by most medical standards. He felt that she was the reason that Lieutenant Allan was able to recover so quickly.

Dr. Meyer wanted to see more of Sherry, to be sure, but he was also either fascinated or puzzled, he wasn't sure which, by David's ramblings about the future. He wanted to learn more about what David thought he knew about the future and whether or not it was simply a delusional reaction to the TBI.

5

David rapidly continued his recovery process. It was clear to everyone that he was on the mend, more than what was expected. He had already scanned enough magazines, television programs, and the daily Washington Posts newspapers to realize that he was currently living in 1991, and not where he expected to be in 2003.

He gathered tidbits of facts that interested him from the leisure section of the newspaper. The movie critics wrote about, *An Angel at my Table*; *Dying Young*, with Julia Roberts; and *Rocketeer*.

The N.Y. Times Best-selling list of books included, *Oh, the Places You'll Go*! By Dr. Seuss; *Immortality* by Milan Kundera; and *The Commanders* by Bob Woodard. Finally, he looked over the music hits of the day and noticed that the "Smashing Pumpkins had debuted their album, "Unusual heat," with the song, "Only Heaven Knows." David's eyes stopped when he read, "Bohemian Rhapsody/These are the Days of our Lives," by Queen and "Do you remember," by Phil Collins.

"I don't know," he muttered.

Sherry walked into the room with some coffee, her mere presence emitting a ray of sunlight that engulfed the room. "Good morning, honey. Coffee?"

"Yes, but first…"

David wasn't able to complete his request for a kiss because she had already leaned forward to give him one, being careful not to spill the contents in the Styrofoam cup that she still held.

"Ummmm, that's the sugar to go in my coffee, right?"

Sherry laughed and sat carefully on David's bed. "You betcha!"

David happily scooted over to make room. "How about the creamer?"

"That will wait," she added before reaching over to kiss him again. This time, she kept her arms around his neck and did not want to let go.

David did not mind at all and he leaned his head softly into her face. "I could stay like this forever," David said, finally breaking the silence.

'Me too, honey!"

Dr. Meyer's entrance into the room interrupted their cozy state. He was followed by a different nurse, another Major. "Garret," was written on her black name tag, pinned above her right breast.

Sherry jumped up from the bed as Dr. Meyer approached them. "Please, sit down. You're fine. I just came to check up on you both and to deliver the good news that we will try to get you out of here before the end of the day!"

Both David and Sherry could not contain their excitement. "Yes!" David shouted while raising a fist in the air.

"YEA!" Sherry screamed while leaning back towards David and giving him a huge bear hug.

"Major Garret will assist you with the discharge details and you both have the information packet containing all of the instructions with you already, I believe."

"Yes, Dr. Meyers! Thank you so much for everything!" Sherry had jumped up to give the Colonel a hug of appreciation. He sheepishly allowed her to.

"I'll leave the two of you alone; to let you celebrate this moment."

Dr. Meyers left the room, glancing back over his should for a brief moment and then moved swiftly away.

Moments later, Dr. Meyers sat alone in his (describe) office on the (what floor) of Walter Reed. He was intrigued by Sherry, her personality, looks; the whole way she handled herself. He would really miss her presence. More intriguing to the neurosurgeon however, was the information he gathered from Major Allan during several of their "skull" sessions. Dr. Meyers opened his file cabinet, marked, "recent," pulled out a folder with the name, "Lieutenant David Allan," plopped it on his desk in front of him, and then began pouring over his notes.

"We were in Iraq to drive out Saddam for his alleged role in the 911 attacks," Lieutenant Allan had answered.

"What were the 911 attacks again?"

"That's when commercial airliners were commandeered by terrorists and then flown into the Trade Center Towers in York City and the Pentagon in D.C."

"This was in 2001?"

"Yes sir, 2001."

"Iraq was responsible for planning these attacks?"

"Not entirely, they became a target in the 'War on Terrorism,' but Osama Bin Laden and Al-Qaeda were the primary perpetrators. They were located in Afghanistan."

Dr. Meyers continued to read back over his recorded conversations and jotted down more notes.

"Fascinating stuff," he said aloud to himself. "Osama Bin Laden; who is that?"

After 90 minutes of reading and scribbling notes, Dr. Meyers neatly placed the documents back into the folder, looked it over a few seconds, and then placed it into a different filing cabinet marked, 'Archives."

Major Garret began a long conversation with Sherry as David watched. "I get to go home!" He thought to himself. "But what will happen when I get there? Would my relationship with Robby and Jenny be the same as I remembered it to be 12 years ago?"

David's thoughts tossed like ocean waves crashing against the shore, over and over with varying degrees of intensity. "Did I tell Dr. Meyers too much? Does he even believe me?"

He wondered if he would make the same choices as he did when he lived in 1991. One thing for certain, David was ready! He was ready to go home and start fresh with whatever he would face, perhaps for the second time around. Maybe he could prevent the "bad" and take advantage of the "good" based on what he knew from the past. David began hoping beyond hope, that this new world he was in would provide great opportunity and was no dream after all.

6

"DAAADY!!" Both Robby and Jenny bounded from the front porch, both of their grandmother's right behind them, and ran forward to Lieutenant David Allan as he slowly stepped out of the passenger side of their Plymouth Minivan.

David held out his arms unable to contain a flashy big smile. "Heeey, come here you t...'thump." They already dove into their father's waiting arms, nearly knocking him for a loop.

"Be careful!" Sherry started, but David was already holding onto them as if they were long lost children, embracing them more so then he remembered doing before; many years before.

"Look at your head," David said to Robby while rubbing the top of it.

"He got his head shaved to be 'hardcore' just for you," Sherry added.

"Daddy, you know what? I can ride a bike now, wanna see?" Jenny said excitedly.

"Yeah, show daddy how you ride, Jenny," Sherry said.

"Jenny, show daddy your new dance too!" Robby added as they both started laughing.

"Okay, I want to see both," David said.

David's mother waited for the appropriate time before she stepped in for her set of hugs followed by Sherry's mother.

"We were all surely praying for you!" Mary told him

As if on cue, Jenny and Robby already had their bikes ready in the front yard when David stood talking with the three ladies.

"Daddy, look! Jenny was riding fast with Robby right behind her. She had her tongue curled in determination, eyes focused on the road ahead of her.

"Alright, girl, that was great!"

The three adults clapped as she got down and took a deep breath then smiled to the acknowledgements.

"Do your dance," Robby shouted.

Jenny placed one hand on her hip as if she was prepared to scold a spoiled brat, held out her other hand like she was about to thumb a ride, and then began shaking her right hip, left hip, and then right hip again.

Everybody erupted with laughter. "Cool dance, girl!"

The small family reunion was not entirely like David remembered but he recalled that Jenny did learn to ride a bike while he was away and that she had demonstrated both her new bike riding skills and her dancing gig.

The house seemed to be set up the way he remembered, yellow ribbons tied around the two trees in the front yard and all six of the front porch columns wrapped in yellow ribbon. Inside looked the same as he remembered also. The formal dining room was immediately to the left just before entering the family room. There was the easy chair against the wall facing in the direction of the fireplace at the far end of the room against the back. He had almost forgotten about this house on Arrow Ridge way, just off of Bingham Drive where they spent a year before moving to on-post housing. It was a quaint 3-bedroom house with a nice large front porch with swings.

The entire normal daily life sort of things appeared to be running its course normally, dinner preparation, eating, clean-up, wrestling with the kids, watching a little TV, and reading to the kids before bed and so forth. What David really wondered was how things would be after everything was settled and he and Sherry were in bed together for the first time after his "Time travel experience?"

Finally the time came when the two of them laid quietly in bed, the lights off and the house quiet. They did not spend much time together in D.C. Sherry wanted to fly home the day she found out that David was to be released and was somehow able to arrange a flight out the next morning.

David reached over to turn on a nightstand lamp, and set it for low. "I at least want to look into your beautiful eyes, babe."

Sherry smiled and placed her hand lovingly on his face. "I really missed you, honey!"

They looked into each other's eyes for a moment and then their lips moved together. Sherry's lips were as soft and sweet as he remembered. David felt the real sensation of her touch and their kissing became more passionate with every passing second. "This was no dream!" The reality of their expressed love engulfed his whole being and dream or not, David felt like he was in paradise.

7

David concentrated on the sights, places, and people around him, wondering whether or not everything was familiar or if he could recollect any event in the process. Often he would ask himself, "Should I be doing this? Did I do that before?" There was some confusion at times as to what were the real memories verses the perceived, "should be,' actions to take based on what he learned over the next 12 years.

Although there were many familiar instances that David seemed to recall vividly, there was not total control of his decisions based on the mere fact that certain portions of his "new" journey did not appear to be heading in the exact direction as he remembered. This became evident almost immediately after coming out of his 3-month coma when told of the events concerning his return home from Desert Storm. That account of the mine exploding beneath their Humvee resulting in the death of SSG Schmidt, simply did not take place on the first go-around. He still wondered if the whole thing was a very realistic dream.

On his first day back to duty at the unit, he remembered all of the officers and soldiers.

"Hey, good morning, sir!" SSG Broom said while standing up with an extended hand.

"Good morning, SSG Broom!" David countered.

Before he could say anything else, a voice echoed down the hall. "Is that Lieutenant Allan I hear?" COL. Smith shouted.

"Yessir, it is!" SSG Broom shouted back.

David heard the footsteps clumping down the old linoleum floor, approaching closer and closer. In seconds, COL. Smith entered the S2 office, followed by Major Surko and a few others.

"Good to see ya, LT!" COL Smith said with an extended hand, just like SSG Broom. He was followed by the others in similar fashion.

"How are you feeling?"

"I feel great, sir and I'm ready to drive on!" David answered enthusiastically.

As the chatter continued David tried to observe and absorb everyone and everything. "It's sort of how I remember our post-Gulf war, as it became known, activities," he thought.

The old two-story chipped-painted, white wooden, building right off All American freeway and Gruber Road was the same as he remembered. He vaguely recalled that he needed to make a sharp left turn onto 9th street to actually arrive to the building. His office looked the same as he remembered; in fact he was not too surprised to find out that he was slotted to replace CPT (Dead) Ringer as the 8th PSYOP Battalion S-2, the staff code for the head security/intelligence section.

As time went on, seemingly in much the same way as it did before, he remembered with increasing interest who was going to make the MLB playoffs and who would win the World Series. This fact, he kept to himself, at least for the time being. The opportunity would come for making the right predictions without bringing too much suspicion on him. He would wait on that. For that matter, he could use the same strategy to predict the Super Bowl opponents and the victors. He remembered all of them from MLB and the NFL. Choosing the right winner would indicate if he indeed was going through some time passage with similar results.

David thought of the strategic possibilities of earning supplemental income, not too much, but enough to live comfortably. Besides the World Series and the Super Bowl, he thought of the stocks that did well through the early and mid '90s, like Dell Computer and American Online. He pursued these thoughts cautiously, not wanting to upset some kind of dimension or level of reality. Putting down wages needed to support a family would have to be discrete and without drawing the attention of Sherry, or anyone else. David would also have to continue living within his means. There would be no way to explain why a Second Lieutenant was living in a mansion and driving a Mercedes. Yes, this whole aspect would need carful contemplation; short term, mid-term, and long-term planning.

Another thought that crossed David's mind and one that needed thoughtful consideration, involved his own position in the military as an intelligence officer. He knew what world events, some catastrophic, that would take place over the next several years. He thought hard on some of the big ones, Hurricane Andrew's destruction on Homestead, Florida; the failed and costly mission for U.S. Army Rangers in Somalia; the unsuccessful attempt to destroy the World Trade Center, at least the first attempt; the bombing in Oklahoma City.

David thought hard to piece together the specifics leading to these events based on the information released after the facts. Could he prevent such events? He wondered. Maybe God was giving him another chance to prevent, fix, or correct something. Would he even want to step in to prevent them? Would that keep him from ever learning the truth as to why and how he abruptly left 2003? Maybe he did not want to know. Maybe it was even the end for him. There was so much to think about. He had time. Not much, but he had time. He would take things one day at a time and move forward like everybody else in his new/old surroundings.

The summer of 1991 came and went much like David remembered it. There was the travel to Salem, Virginia, Sherry's hometown. He would go to his own place of birth, Baltimore, Maryland, with a side trip to Gettysburg so that the kids could experience a taste of history. They even stopped and visited the small town of Schuylkill Haven, Pennsylvania to visit an old Army buddy, Dan, from the 80's, and his family. Dan was the same old muscle-bound wrestler that he remembered. They even went fishing, an event that David recalls because it was the first fish that Jennifer ever caught.

Disney World, Epcot, and a trip to David's grandmother's mobile home in Venice, Florida rounded out the traveling for the summer. Both of Sherry's sisters got married in Lakeland, Florida during the summer so the theme park adventure's coincided with the weddings. Fort Bragg celebrated the 4th of July with concerts and fireworks. Lee Greenwood would sing his "God Bless the USA" hit song to the cheering throng.

The other events that came back to life included the change-of-command between his old commander, COL. Smith to the new one, LTC Vincent. David liked Col. Smith. He was the one who gave him his present position as the S2. They served together during Desert Storm and David recalls the time he had to flush COL. Smith's eyes with water when gasoline from a generator splashed into his face while on his way to the front. Now David wondered if that event ever took place.

Sherry struggled a bit, trying to find the right teaching gig somewhere in Cumberland County. She had a job teaching kindergarten in the town of Spring Lake, just outside of the post but the school had to let one of the kindergarten teachers go because of cuts. The school decided to keep the lady who screamed at the kids all day because of her minority status and the quota's that the county had to keep. Sherry was livid when she discovered the reason for her dismissal.

The most devastating event was when Sherry's mom went into a coma during the month of August. Mary was scheduled to have a simple should operation and then recoup at their house in Fayetteville. Remembering that she would indeed slip into a coma in post-op because of an aneurysm, David strongly suggested that she put off surgery until another time and he gave numerous reasons, short of telling the whole family that she would slip into a coma during post-op, why she should not have the surgery. Mary went through with the surgery anyway and everything took place just as it had before.

Sherry took this very hard. David remembered this as well. Could he have stopped it? What if they listened to him and did not go through with the surgery? Would the coma come in a different way, maybe while on the road? David could not bear the thought that he may have been able to prevent his mother-in-law's state.

Sherry's family, consisting of her father, who was a diabetic-related amputee, her brother, Jeff, and her three sisters made the correct decision to remove any life-support from Mary. They each said their good-bye's in their own terms and waited for the worse.

What David neglected to tell everyone, purposely, was that she would go on to live for another 4 months, still in a coma, before dying of pneumonia just before Christmas. It was a dreadful thought and he put it out of his mind. Let the events run its course. "How could I possibly stop the results now?" He wondered.

8

Although being at the Organization Day activities that included an evening at the club wearing Dress Blues was supposed to be a celebrated occasion, David could tell that Sherry was still troubled deep down by her mother's condition. This was to be expected and yet she still displayed an exuberant disposition to all of those officers and wives around her throughout the evening. She held on to David tightly as if she was grasping onto a life that she did not want to slip away while on the dance floor during the ballads.

"Do you think that Doctor Meyers could or even would look into my mother's condition? He did wonders for you, I think." Sherry said between drinks.

"Well, I'm not sure if he could but I can look into the matter."

"Would you please? That would be such a load off my mind, knowing that at least we tried."

"Sure thing, honey. I'll try to contact him when I get into the office on Monday morning and see what I can find out."

"Thanks so much, dear." Sherry took a sip from her champagne glass, watching David in the process.

Her eyes, transfixed on David's, sparkled from the reflective overhead lights above the shining rim.

"I love you, Sherry." David placed his hands across the table in front of him and Sherry reached down her left hand to squeeze his for a few seconds and then left her palm on top of his hand.

During a break period, while many of the ladies disappeared to the powder room or outside for a smoke break, LTC Vincent sat down next to David.

"I heard about all that you went through and what your wife is going through now."

"Yes sir, it has been a difficult year."

"Well, you have my support and I intend to keep you as my '2.'

"Thank you, sir. I certainly appreciate that opportunity!"

"If there is anything that I or my wife, Sabrina, can do, never hesitate to ask."

"Thanks again, sir. I appreciate that."

LTC Vincent started to get up and move onto something else, but then turned around and continued speaking.

"I've been told that you can provide good intelligence with uncanny accuracy."

David was startled. "Well, I don't know sir, I mean I submit my reports based on the trends and analysis that I receive over the net, but I don't know how accurate it turns out to be."

"You mean you haven't received any feedback about your input?"

"Well, yes sir. I've been told that I give good information and that I'm doing a good job; to keep up the good work."

LTC Vincent chuckled. "Yes indeed. You give very good information. Your analytical assessment concerning the dismantling of the U.S.S.R and the failed coup attempt prior to any of it taking place was spot on!"

"I was just making a prediction based on the 'reading of the tea leaves,' sir."

"Uh huh, that's what I'm talking about. "I'll talk to you later; I gotta get over here and do some mingling."

"Roger that, sir."

9

Major David Allan could sometimes be found hanging out discretely in various clubs, such as the "Cadillac Ranch" on Fort Bragg Road and the recently opened, "Dallas of Fayetteville" on Owen Drive. There were those "official" Commander's Call on Friday afternoon as well that was always planned in a side room in the Officer's Club. Drinks at the bar were sure to follow.

David's interest was not in drinking so much, nor was it in trying to pick up members of the opposite sex. No, he was quite content with Sherry and everything he wanted in a woman. David had no trouble finding those who were willing to part with their money for friendly bets on baseball and football games.

With the Pirates leading the National League Championship series, 3 games to 2, David willing bet that the Braves would pull off games 6 and 7. He even called the score for game 6, but declined to do so for game 7. It was during game 6 with the Braves up 1-0 and the Pirates coming to bat in the bottom of the 9th that David's table drew a crowd. Alejandro Pena replaced Tommy Gregg pitching and Gary Varsho came in to bat for Doug Drabek.

"Well, Allan, let's see if you get this one." Captain Nelson chided.

Jack Buck could barely be heard above the noise, "Two balls and two strikes on Varsho. Here's the pitch, Line drive base hit up the center…

"Hahaha doesn't look good for you, my man."

David just smiled, and took a swig of the drink in front of him. "It ain't over yet, Captain."

Orlando Merced batted for Gary Redus and sent Varsho over to second base on a sacrifice bunt. One out.

Bell came up next and promptly lined to right field on the first pitch.

"Whew, you were lucky on that one."

The next batter was Andy Van Slyke, one of the Pirates best hitters. Buck could be heard a little better above the clatter, "No balls and a strike; here's the pitch. A wild pitch; Varsho is taking third!"

There was some cheering in the background.

"$100.00 says he strikes out!" David suddenly announced.

"You got that much?" someone yelled behind him.

Before he could answer, Captain Nelson said, "He's good for it, I'll vouch for him."

"You're on!" the young man said, a stranger to David.

"Anybody else?" David asked.

There were a few more takers and the crowd grew larger around them.

Captain Nelson broke into a wide grin. Good thing there are more than 3 of us here tonight.

"David acted edgy. It was quite possible that he may be wrong about this whole idea.

Buck could be heard more clearly now since the room grew quiet. "One ball and two strikes on Van Slyke. Here's the pitch. "STRIKE three called as Andy stands watching and the game is over! The Braves are still alive!"

There were some bystanders not looking too pleased when David gathered the pot, but the presence of more than a few of his Psyop buddies circling around him, staved off any attempt to start a ruckus, at least for now.

"You boy's might wanna get outta here now." The bartender deadpanned.

"We're gone!" David answered and left abruptly with his latest winnings heading straight to his car with Captain Nelson, Lieutenant Winsted, and Captain Baily in tow.

"That was awesome, how do you do it? You're coming tomorrow night, right?"

"Not a chance," David answered. "It's our 10th anniversary and I plan on going somewhere quite nice."

"So, who's going to win tomorrow night's game?" Lieutenant Winsted asked.

"I'll give you some of tonight's winnings. Be sure to bet on the Braves to take it." David peeled away a few bills and handed them to Winsted.

"But I wouldn't come back to this place." David added.

While correctly predicting the Braves to win in 7 games and then picking the Twins to take the Braves in 7 games in the World Series, including a prediction that game 7 would end 1-0, David eventually opened a separate bank account telling Sherry that this would be the investment account based on the small amount of money he put into the Dell stocks. Most of the deposits came from his uncanny knack of predicting the winning and losing teams however and Sherry was clueless as to the amount that was being amassed.

If she would want to inquire at some point, David could easily tell her that Dell is doing much better than he anticipated. Still, he could not just go out and lay money down for a Mercedes.

Sherry did not seem too concerned about any additional revenue, especially since David kept most of it a secret. She innocently inquired about David's pre-planned sitters and his exquisite taste when he took her to the Italian Ristorante for dinner and a night stay at the Siena Hotel in Chapel Hill. Not that she was complaining. She needed to get away and unwind. Her appreciation towards David's attempts to get Dr. Meyers involved in her mother's case meant a lot to her.

Dr. Meyers made an effort to visit Sherry's mother and eventually consult with her doctor at the nursing home in Salem, Virginia. It was not clear to Sherry why Dr. Meyers wanted to go out of his way but had her own ideas. David thought that he was still intrigued by his own case and the resulting success. Although only Dr. Meyers is the only one who really knew, it could have been the combination of the most interesting case that he ever had as a Neurosurgeon and one of the most interesting and beautiful woman that he ever met.

Unfortunately, the prognosis was not as good as the one he had for David several months before. Still, Sherry was extremely grateful for David's efforts to help her mother. She just wanted to put everything behind her for now, and look back on the past 10 years that she had just spent with David. She wanted to reflect on the two beautiful children, Robby and Jenny, that they conceived together, and how much the two of them meant to her. Sherry consoled herself that she still had the three of them in her life and that life itself, would indeed go on.

1991 had been a difficult year for Sherry. Her husband went off to war in the gulf, not knowing when or even if he would return. David did of course, but not as the same person he was when he left. Besides his obvious near fatal injuries, there was something peculiar about him that she could not fully grasp. He was still her David, though, the same man she fell in love with ten years before when they met on a mission base in Ecuador.

While David was recuperating from his trauma, Sherry's father had his leg amputated from lack of blood circulation. This was due to diabetes related complications that was not appropriately cared for. Then, shortly after David's recovery, her mother, Mary, had an aneurysm in post-op after a routine shoulder surgery. She would never recover and eventually succumb to pneumonia four months later.

David decided that the family needed to get away for a vacation. What better place to go then a far off country, away from danger, where they first met. Sherry, David, Robby, and Jennifer were visiting David's brother, Mike, sister-in-law, Robin, and their two small children, Kenny and Diana, for the Christmas Holidays. Mike and his family followed his father's footsteps as a missionary and ended up in the same country where he previously served. Maybe the time away from the hustle and bustle would be just what Sherry needed. David did recall that when they made this trip in the past, that is if this whole thing wasn't still a dream, that although Sherry was quite depressed about her mother, she was very thankful to be away from everything and "fall off the world map" for a period of time.

David remembered correctly and the change of pace was exactly what Sherry needed. Ecuador was a picturesque country. The city where they would spend most of their time, Quito, was surrounded by enormous snow-capped peaks jutting from the mountainous Andean range. Mike was in fact a semi-professional climber, equipped with the latest mountain-climbing gear, such as the picks, spiked shoes, etc. available.

To the east of the city, the altitude sloped downward towards the Amazon basin. For two nights, both families traveled together to the jungle with stops along the way at an enclave consisting of natural springs. This whole trip was good for Sherry and exciting for the kids. It was a good way to end a bad year. To David, everything seemed to be falling in place the right way. For Sherry, surely, 1992 would be a better year. David knew in his heart that it would be; that is if he did everything right and stayed the course. It just had to be.

10

During the following year of 1992, Second Lieutenant, David Allan was promoted to First Lieutenant. Sherry was there during the small ceremony that was conducted outside the 8th Psyop Headquarter building. LTC Vincent and Sherry did the honors of pinning on the silver bars in place of the "butter bars," so named for its yellowish appearance.

The formation of troops consisted of the enlisted ranks, numbering around 40 or so. The other officers were standing around in various spots behind the formation and to the left flank. David felt proud of his first promotion as an officer. It was a similar feeling to the time he was promoted to a Sergeant in 1983.

Both he and Sherry gave a short speech and then it was back to work for most. David and LTC Vincent wore their Class A's uniform which was not required by anybody else in the unit. He and Sherry were invited to a lunch at the club with LTC Vincent and his wife who also attended the promotion. The four of them left together shortly after the ceremony, which was timed appropriately to end close to the lunch hour.

LTC Vincent had been impressed by David's intelligence analysis. He had predicted the failed coup in Russia and the subsequent declaration of independence by various nations that were formerly part of the Soviet Union. The Battalion commander often called David into his office late in the afternoons, just to chat about the world events and what David thought would come about from the circumstances.

It was during these afternoon chats, that David carefully predicted what would happen in Los Angeles later in the year in the event of a not guilty verdict in the Rodney King case. Unknown to the L.A. Police, King was caught on film while being beaten up by them when King resisted arrest in 1991. This would cause racial riots to break out in south central L.A. and eventually lead to several days of rioting. David was careful not to divulge the fact that he knew what the outcome of the verdict would be.

David's uncanny knack of sharing accurate information included the prediction that Bosnia and Herzegovina would secede from Yugoslavia. Although LTC Vincent was not too familiar with some of these names at the time he grew increasingly interested in the outcome.

The one predictive analysis that David gave at the weekly staff meeting was when the subject of a "Humanitarian" invasion of Somalia was in the works because of the severe famine caused by warlords and civil war. LTC Vincent took a keen interest in learning more and asked David to stop by his office after the meeting.

"So, what can you tell me about this Somalia business? You know we have been asked to send a small element therein support."

"Yes sir, I did hear that."

LTC Vincent looked at him intently. "Go on."

"Well sir, I don't believe that it will end well for our soldiers and we will eventually pull out of the country with our tails between our legs."

LTC Vincent didn't laugh. "Why?"

"Well sir, it's kind of hard to explain but the bottom line is I don't believe that our command is fully aware of the array of trained terrorists that exist there, especially in Mogadishu. They are trained in irregular, asymmetric warfare in urban areas and I believe that we will go there not fully prepared."

"I want a written report on my desk by COB tomorrow. Be sure to add some specific background information on their enemy forces that we might encounter."

David squirmed in his chair slightly and while his thoughts scrambled for a recollection of group names and key individuals, he quickly answered, "Yes sir! Consider it done!"

LTC Vincent got out of his chair, rubbed his chin and said, "This is some good stuff. I don't think that anybody has viewed courses of actions that may involve terrorist groups and urban warfare. What was that word you used, Asymmetric warfare?

"Yes sir, it…"

"I never heard that term before. Is this a new MI term? Give me the scoop.

"It isn't used officially really, but I believe that it will be used more often to describe the type of warfare that we will most likely be involved with in the future, especially now that the Soviet Union has all but dissolved.

"Interesting. Be prepared to give a quick brief at the Group level on Friday."

"Yes sir!"

"I know you can handle it and will do alright. Just be sure to have that report on my desk tomorrow and I'll review it first. You'll be standing by in case I have any questions."

"Yes sir!"

"Good job, Davy. I'll talk to you tomorrow."

"Thank you, sir."

David stopped by a phone booth across the parking lot from the Battalion building before going home for the evening. He pulled out a piece of paper, placed a dollar's worth of quarters in the slot and began dialing. After a couple of rings, the man's voice answered excitedly.

"Hello, Las Vegas Sports casino, can I help you?"

"What are the odds on Toronto Blue Jays winning the Word Series this year?"

There was a brief hesitation. "500 to 1 to win it all."

"Could you look at my account for Davy Crockett, 312-908-766, and place $1500.00 on the Blue Jays?"

"You sure about this, Mr. Crockett?"

"Yes, I think so."

"Alright, but you only have $2,000.00 in your account and I would hate for you to have to lose over half of it for nothing."

"That's okay; I'll get more in there soon."

Okay, consider it done. You'll have the written confirmation and details in the mail."

"Okay, thanks."

David though in his head a moment after placing the receiver back on the hook. "250 grand! Wow, what will I do with it?"

Later in the year, David's predictive analysis continued to impress more and more of the brass. The Group commander called him to his office one day after briefing everyone that Hurricane Andrew would cause considerable damage to south Florida when the Hurricane was still in the Atlantic before warnings were issued in August. David was careful not to tell anyone that Homestead AFB would nearly be demolished after taking a direct hit killing about a dozen people and leaving a couple hundred thousand homeless. He did pass on a warning up his chain-of-command that the Air Force personnel in Homestead, Florida may want to take extra precautions in preparation for what David said was most likely going to be a category 5 Hurricane.

David had also stated during a staff briefing that it would not surprise him if the 82nd Airborne and elements from the 4th Psyop Group or Civil Affairs would be deployed to Homestead for administering aid and relief, once the facts were out that Homestead was indeed devastated.

The most exciting news to David, which he kept to himself, was the fact that the Toronto Blue Jays did win the World Series and the payoff was cause to celebrate! This he did with a weekend away from the base, alone with Sherry. The getaway was a surprise but David arranged everything, including the sitters for Robby and Jenny.

"Wow, this is nice!" Sherry exclaimed while looking at the plush suite at the newly opened Renaissance SouthPark Hotel, in Charlotte.

"I thought you'd like it."

Sherry stopped gazing at the room and looked at David. "And we can afford this?"

"Of course..."

"Without going into debt, I mean."

"Yes, I used money from my investment account, we're doing fine."

Sherry opened her mouth as if she was going to continue, but abruptly walked over to David and planted a long big kiss instead.

"I love it!"

The two held each other and smiled.

Later that evening, David had reservations at the Bernardin's Restaurant, a favorite among locals. David caught several men stealing a glance at Sherry as she glided to her table wearing a new royal blue, one sleeve, and long evening dress with a high leg slit. He wore a casual navy suit and the two of them sat together by the window enjoying each other's company.

The restaurant was lined with just the right amount of mirrors to make the place look a bit roomier without appearing like a carnival. There were numerous floral bouquets that looked freshly cut from the Carolinian landscape displayed on the tar-heel blue banquettes.

David's focus was on Sherry's beautiful eyes that never ceased to captivate him, those eyes and her smile. He was oblivious to those sitting around them, unaware of any talk that may have been directed towards them. Not that it mattered anyway. He and Sherry both relished the moment and together savored their Fried Calamari Appetizer, which was followed by the Grilled Pepper Crusted Filet Mignon.

"So, just what are you investing in these days?"

David could tell by her smile and the fact that she reached over across the white tablecloth table to hold his hand that she really did not care about the details, but had in fact grown accustomed to David's generosity displayed towards her.

"I have expanded into the latest technology in phones, Palm Pilots and other personal assistants."

"Palm pilots?"

"Yes, they are handheld personal digital assistants that I believe will one day evolve into smartphones. Basically, a computer in the palm of your hand."

"That sounds interesting, David. Is this really the wave of the future…well, it must be. Look at you… and me!"

"It's working out okay, Sherry. I mean…"

"I was thinking, pardon the interruption. If this continues to go so well, maybe you should think about getting out of the Army."

David was surprised by Sherry's comment. She had been the driving force behind him leaving the enlisted ranks to become an officer and then urging him to move forward until retirement.

"Well, I don't know, Sherry…"

"Just a thought. I almost lost you last year. She bit her lip. The kids and I would not know what to do without you."

"I'll give it some thought, babe, but things are going real well at the unit also, and you know, investments, they could be here today and gone tomorrow."

"That's true, I suppose.

Two waiters appeared, one to remove their empty plates and the other appearing with a dessert cart. After making their selections, their conversation turned towards more trivial matters, such as how good the dessert tasted and how they should walk it off in a nearby park.

"Then we can continue our romantic evening back in our 'fancy-dancy' plushy room at the Renaissance."

For the first time that evening, David looked around him at the other patrons. He felt a bit sheepish since Sherry's announcement was a bit above ear-shot.

Then they both started to laugh.

11

Besides being promoted to a First Lieutenant in 1992, David was also elected to the Board of Directorates at the local church he attended, Calvary Assembly, on Fort Bragg Road. This coincided with a move from their quaint house off of Bingham Drive to junior officer housing on post. David missed the house off post, but Sherry wanted the conveniences that came with on-post officer housing so the move was made with their new residence being on Normandy Drive, just below the hill from the outdoor swimming pool on Ardennes.

The new house included a decent size backyard and David put up the authorized chain-linked fence because the promise to get a new puppy for Robby and Jennifer after the move necessitated the labor. Everyone thought that the new dog, Rusky, so named by Jennifer, would turn into the size of a horse based on his big paws. It wasn't until a veterinarian asked Sherry how old the dog was during a check-up that his current size was as large as he would get.

"What, you're kidding me!" Sherry said laughing.

"No, he has reached his height although he will most likely fill out some more."

Sherry laughed again. "What kind of dog is this then?"

The veterinarian even chuckled. "It looks like it may have some shepherd and Corgi in it."

"Corgi? What is that?"

"It's a collie type of herding dog predominately found in England. I may have some pictures. Let me check."

Sherry looked at Rusky with a mixture of relief, since she did not want a big dog to begin with, and a reassuring smile. Don't worry, boy, we'll take care of you. I should say, your daddy will."

The most significant move for David was the change in units within Fort Bragg. The Military Intelligence Branch told David that his best career move would be to try and find a spot in the 525th MI Brigade and work directly within an Intelligence unit.

David did not like the idea very much but knew that it was going to come. He just couldn't tell anybody. He liked where he was within the PSYOP world and he liked who he worked for, both LTC Vincent and the Executive officer, Major Randolph. Additionally, he was starting to get noticed at the higher Group levels with the PSYOP/Civil Affairs arena and was invited to particular VIP functions.

"Branch wants you to move? Give a name and number and I'll call them."

David was a bit hesitant to let LTC Vincent get involved but it was proper protocol to let him know what his branch was trying to push for his career. Knowing that he in fact made this move was also a bit risky if too many people got involved in trying to prevent the move.

"Sir, although I really like it here and would rather stay, I believe that they are just looking out for my best career interest. You know how it is with the conventional mind set. PSYOP just hasn't hit their radar screen yet."

"Yeah, tell me about it. I hear you, Davy. I had to jump through hoops with my branch just to get into this type of work. Alright, if you're okay with it, I don't want to hinder your professional development. I sure hate to lose you though."

"Yes sir, I would rather stay, myself. I believe in time however, PSYOP will play a more dominant role in future wars."

"Asymmetric, you once said, right?"

"Yes sir, asymmetric."

With the help from the MI branch, David found a new unit that would welcome him with open arms.

"This is great timing Lieutenant Allan!" CPT Metzger said. We're about to lose our XO and quite frankly, we did not have anybody legit that we could think of to replace him. He'll be a huge loss for us."

"Yes sir, I look forward to coming over and stepping right in."

"You'll fit right in. Your ORB and OER look great! I can't wait to have you on board."

David met and was interviewed by CPT Metzger after an arranged phone call by the MI branch was made to the 525 MI Brigade S-1, CPT Larson. Larson contacted Metzger and paved the way for David's smooth transition as an XO in Charley Company, 319th MI Battalion, of the 525th MI Brigade. Like the 8th PSYOP unit that he just left, it was also an airborne unit, meaning that he would still be able to make the extra bonus for jumping out of planes.

While everything seemed to be falling in place the way he remembered it up to this point, there was that part of his new life that made him a little nervous; putting money down on certain investments and calling winners of the World Series and Super Bowl. His favorite money making game was when the Houston Oilers were beating the Buffalo Bills, 35-3 during a playoff game on the 3rd of January,

1993. This was when David decided to place money wherever he could on a comeback victory by Buffalo. The Bills, of course, did come back to win in overtime, 41-38. By David's estimation, his separate, and very private account, contained nearly $800,000. He was still being cautious in not trying to gain undue attention. And this was one secret that he had to keep…even from Sherry.

12

The sign at the front gate read, "TENCAP complex." TENCAP was the acronym for the Tactical Exploitation of National Capabilities. Although this was his new place of business, signal and imagery type of intelligence was not David's favorite area of intelligence gathering. He preferred the HUMINT aspect, which involved Human Intelligence.

TENCAP had the purpose of exploiting tactical and national space systems by integrating these capabilities into rapid operational military decision-making for the XVIII Airborne Corps. The systems on hand at the complex provided the commander with access to national assets, such as other national intelligence agencies and consumers.

David's role as the Executive Officer focused more on the day-to-day operations of the unit itself. He was responsible for supervising all of the company's vehicles. It was up to David to establish an efficient maintenance program. His other duties included the "Cup & Flower" fund, Family Support, and a variety of other responsibilities that were given him by the company commander, CPT Harrington.

As for significant world events, newly elected President Bill Clinton was inaugurated on the 20th of January. Life in the military was sure to change under his administration. It was a surprise to most that he was able to defeat former President George Bush, but as usual, David predicted the outcome and even suggested that President Bush was not trying hard enough and wondered aloud if he really wanted another term in office.

Since David was not directly involved with any of the ongoing intelligence, of any kind, he mostly suggested outcomes and warnings to anyone who would listen. But as expected, not too many listened to a First Lieutenant, at least, not anymore. LTC Vincent took a keen interest in David's ability to call accurate intelligence analysis. David felt more appreciated there than with his current unit.

David made a call to his former boss in early February. "Hello, sir, this is Lieutenant Allan. How are you?"

"Hey Davey, how's everything over there in the MI world?"

"Well sir, it's slow from my perspective."

"We miss you over here, when are you coming back?"

"Probably not possible, sir. However, I remember how you liked talking about lintel analysis with me and thought maybe we could get together sometime in the near future at your convenience."

"Yeah, that would be great, Davey. I'm heading down range for a while. Maybe when I get back we can catch up on old times."

"Okay sir, I'll contract you later.

"Hey listen, I gotta run. Thanks for calling me."

"Okay sir, bye."

David began to realize that there was not much of a market for whatever intelligence he possessed from memory, at least not in his former or present unit. He contemplated his options and wondered just who would understand and appreciate his insight and take him seriously. Who could he reveal his knowledge to about the upcoming car bomb that would explode in a garage beneath one of the World Trade Centers in New York?

All of the major news networks carried the top story: A huge explosion, apparently of a car bomb in an underground garage, collapsed walls and floors beneath New York's two tallest buildings. Fires from the blast sent smoke up more than 100 stories, and a power cutoff trapped hundreds for hours. The explosion gouged a large, twisted cavern out of four underground levels tearing away concrete walls and leaving steel girders bent like pipe cleaners. Officials stated that the bomb was placed perfectly to damage the entire infrastructure of the building.

Images of the two World Trade Center buildings crumpling to the ground in a thick cloud of smoke ran through David's mind. This was the first moment when he realized that he might even be able to prevent such a disaster as those that took place on September 11, 2001. But who would listen? If he provided the details, he could even be implicated as a co-conspirator. He had to think this through. There was still time. But this problem needs further exposure, before it's too late.

David would need to be at the right unit, talking to the right people. Maybe he could head it off at the pass by sending intelligence agencies on the trail of the terrorists during their early planning stage. While mulling over various ideas in his own head, and his alone, the answer came calling to him.

"Steve, this is Ray. Do you remember me from San Antonio?"

David knew what that introduction was, but he nearly forgot completely about "Ray."

"Ah, yes, Ray. How have you been? I haven't heard from you in quite a while?"

"Doing well, thanks. Say, listen, can we meet sometime next week?"

"Sure, I can make time. When and where?"

"Have you ever been to Pinehurst?"

"Not that I can remember."

"That's okay. It's easy to get to from where you are. Let's meet at the Magnolia Inn on 65 Magnolia road in Pinehurst next Thursday at 7:00 pm. Will that work?'

David was scribbling on a piece of note paper that he found on his desk. "65 Magnolia Road in Pinehurst, right?"

"Yes, you got it. Is the time good?'

"Sure, 7:00 next Thursday."

"Alright. See you then. Looking forward to it."

"Okay, likewise. Later."

David set the phone down and thought back to his relationship with Ray and the other guy, "what was his name again… oh yeah, Stan."

He met the two of them in 1987 when he was departing from the Army as an enlisted soldier to attend college and pursue a commission through ROTC. David considered them to be "handlers" or liaison officers" during a chess match, so-to-speak, involving him and a Soviet officer that approached him in Berlin the year before. Like a good soldier, David reported the incident but rather than patting him on the back and telling him, "Great work," they asked him if he would be willing to meet with the officer and find out what he wanted.

After several pre-briefings with the Americans, David entered East Berlin, as a tourist, and met in a clandestine manner with the Soviet officer at a restaurant. David remembered most of the discussion revolving around "our great leaders, Gorbechev and Reagan."

Vladimir, at least the name he gave David when they first met, was wearing civilian attire, typical for an East German on a Saturday afternoon, light-layered olive-colored shirt and jacket. He was right where he said he would be, around the corner on Alexander Platz.

"Good afternoon," he began. "I was wondering if you would come or not, but I am very glad that you did. Have you had something to eat yet?"

Jerry, the American agent in Berlin told David not to eat anything before the meeting because the Russian would most likely take him out to a restaurant. "No, I haven't," I replied.

"Good, I know of a place that serves real good food. Let's go there to sit, relax and talk."

"Okay," David answered, and then followed him at a short distance behind as instructed, since he was still wearing his military Class A uniform.

They entered a plain looking building from the outside, but decorated nicely inside. Vladimir asked for a particular table in the back and the two of them had the small room to themselves. His nature was jovial, even as he ordered his food and offered suggested items, translating the German into his well-spoken English for David. He certainly was not the stereotype Soviet officer David had envisioned during all his years of military training and indoctrination. As the waiter collected the menus, Vladimir emphasized that he needed the vodka that he had ordered for both of them to come immediately, before the first course appetizer.

"Well," Vladimir began. "I am so glad you were able to come."

"Like you said, we are allies, right?" David had to sound both convincing and natural, not wanting to tip Vladimir off in any way that he was actually being sent by the Americans. He did want to see Sherry, Robby, and Jenny again and had no desire to be whisked away while in the city of East Berlin.

"That's right, good. I believe that we are on the same side and as you know, your President Reagan and our Prime Minister, Gorbachev are working very well together towards Perestroika. Are you familiar with this?"

"Yes, I hope that it works very well for both of our countries."

"It will! It will, believe me!" Vladimir said with excitement.

Two waiters, dressed in black shirts and black pants with white aprons tied around their waists, came with their salads, and vodka. Vladimir proposed a toast, "To peace between our countries."

"To peace," David added, and downed the shot of vodka while trying to disguise his wincing with a pleasant smile. Before the two waiters moved away, Vladimir made it a point to inform them that they would need another shot of vodka before they came back with our meal.

The vodka came and went, and then came again, this time with the main dish. The two continued discussing world events; the situation in Afghanistan with the Soviet troops and the on-going war between Iran and Iraq. At one point in their conversation, Vladimir added, "We are much alike, just as we were during World War II. We were allies then and should be again soon. Our real enemies are those terrorists in the Middle East. We should be fighting them together."

The food smelled delicious as three waiters laid the plates in front of them... along with two new shot glasses of vodka. They ate, talked in between bites, and enjoyed a typical social meal without any mention as to why David was there or what the Russian wanted from him. This surprised him a bit, but the situation allowed David to relax and act natural more easily.

When one of the waiters came back to check on them, Vladimir requested another shot of vodka for both, their fourth. The Americans had already informed David that the Russian's primary goal would be to get David to trust him so that he would readily agree to meet again at a future date.

"Otherwise," Jerry told him, "Just act natural."

Since, David had a feeling that this type of thing went on more than most soldiers were aware, he had to ask Jerry the obvious question. "So, there's no way that they will hold me there as a spy or something?"

Jerry and his partner, Chad exchanged glances. "That is usually not the case; just remember to act natural."

The afternoon wore on with more pleasantries; Vladimir even asked about David's wife and suggested that maybe a meeting could take place in the future with both wives in attendance. As the plates were being gathered by the waiters, a fourth was taking their order for dessert. Before he could turn away, however, Vladimir requested vodka to come with it. David never really wanted any of the vodka in the first place, but was careful not to do anything that might offend his Soviet host in any manner. He was already beginning to feel its dizzying effects.

They had dessert, and vodka, then coffee, and vodka. In fact, Vladimir put his last shot into his coffee. David's head was spinning. H needed more coffee with the hope of off-setting the liquor.

When the dinner-meeting was finally finished, David somehow remembered the details of the time and date for a future meeting, which he had been instructed to readily accept. The only thing that Vladimir asked him to bring back on the next visit was some hunting magazines. David assured him that he would, that the PX had a lot of them.

Finding his way back to Checkpoint Charley was not an easy task, as the road in front of him seemed to wave back and forth a bit. David wondered what the guards would think in his condition when he attempted to enter back into West Berlin at Checkpoint Charley.

David tried to look away whenever he was asked a question but became more nervous when a couple of young "soldiers" dressed in civilian attire whisked him away from the "uniforms" and told him to park over in a side lot. In the back of his mind David hoped that these guys knew what he was up to and were possibly even working for Jerry and Chad.

One of the young men walked around the car and kept looking at the surrounding area. The other, a short cropped blond in his twenties and sporting designer sunglasses and an overcoat of European fashion walked David to the trunk of my car.

"Open your trunk, please." he demanded politely, with a smile.

David obliged and stepped away, trying not to lose his balance. The young blond man glanced inside briefly and then looked over at him. "Are you alright?"

"Yes, I believe so, thank you."

"You can go," he said with a wry smile. "Are you sure you are alright?"

"Yes."

"Be careful then," he finished as he shut the trunk of David's Opel Manta without looking through it.

"Thanks." David said with relief, hoping that they would offer him a ride to his military housing.

Instead, driving a bit wildly through the streets of West Berlin, David prayed all the way until his wheels screeched to a halt in the complex driveway. "Whew, thank you, Lord!"

Several meetings took place after the first and then continued even after David left the Army the first time to attend college. The MI Branch had to "hand-off" David to the FBI since he was no longer in their jurisdiction. David then met with an FBI agent, introduced as Bill, for the next three years before he re-entered the Army as a Military Intelligence Officer himself.

David assured Sherry about the meeting with Ray and Stan.

"I think they just want to catch up and tell me that the operation is officially over and then wish me good luck."

"I hope that's all it is and I hope that it is over."

"I can't think of anything else they might want from me."

David knew from the past that this was the case, that they would officially seal the record on that operation, once and for all. The Russian's left Berlin after the wall came down and took everything with them that belong to them. David never heard back from his Soviet friend since he last visited him in East Berlin in December of 1987.

Now, David wondered if these guys would be the right ones to divulge some of his knowledge and insight about upcoming events without drawing suspicion from them or the Human Intelligence community that they represented. He would have to craft his words carefully, once again.

David found the Magnolia Inn and went straight to the room 112, the number given him in a coded message from another phone call. David remembered that when discussing sporting events, the score would have significant bearing on the meeting place. David knew that when the voice on the other end of a phone call asked, "Did you catch the Knicks game last night? They won 112-99." Had they lost 112-99, the message would have been, "Did you catch the Knicks game last night? They lost 112-99, and David would have proceeded to room 99. This system worked before.

David walked to the door and struck his fist against the door with the wrap, wrap, wrap, followed by a pause and then wrap, wrap. Ray let him in quickly, while peering over David's shoulder.

"Good to see you again," Stan said while extending his hand towards David.

"Yes, it's been a while," David answered.

Ray extended his hand as well. "Good to see you again."

"How are you?" David responded.

"Good, thanks. Please have a seat."

There was small talk exchanged for a few minutes, then, as remembered, Ray explained that the old Cold war operations will officially come to a close. David even mentioned the fact that he agreed and that the Soviets would probably pull their troops out of Poland by the fall. The two HUMINT officers exchanged glances and chuckled.

Ray also reminded David about consequences of disclosing information concerning the operation or even acknowledging that such interaction even existed. David understood and he signed a form that Ray had prepared in advance. It seemed to David that the two wanted a quick and clean break and then wanted to move on to other things. Before David left the room, he hesitated.

"What do you guys think about the operations in Somalia?"

"We don't have anything to do with it, why?"

"Just wondering. Just for the record, I believe that our forces are up against a lot more than what everyone is saying."

"What do you mean?"

"I believe that General Aideed is more than a warlord. He has urban guerilla warfare training behind him."

"How do you know about General Aideed?" Stan asked.

"Just reading reports and what not."

It was Ray's turn now. "What makes you think he is more than just a ragtag warlord?"

"Just based on information that I read before. Remember, I was an Intel officer with 8th PSYOP once, and the Middle East was our region.

"That's right, he would have that info," ray countered.

"Well, we're not involved but your observation is noted," Stan answered as they stood to see David out the door.

David always enjoyed reading about or listening to world events on the news.

"Russian troops withdraw from Poland," was a headline in mid-September of 1993.

Sadly, the operations conducted by the U.S. army Rangers in Somalia unfolded just the way David remembered they would. The US intervention in Somalia went from a mercy mission to disaster. On October 3rd, more than 500 Somalis, many of them women and children, were killed or injured in fighting involving American troops, in which 16 also died.

The American casualties eventually forced President Bill Clinton to set a withdrawal date for US forces. The warlord, General Mohamed Farah Aideed, proved to have led a disciplined force of urban guerrillas. The elite Ranger forces of the US were caught in a well-orchestrated ambush and suffered 75 per cent casualties. Kofi Annan, the UN under-secretary for peace- keeping, tried to uphold Security Council Resolution 837, which mandated the capture of General Aideed for the killing of 24 Pakistani troops earlier in the summer.

The results of the failed attempt were seen by the American public on television with the image of Chief Warrant Officer Mike Durant, the captured helicopter pilot, lying bloodied and frightened. It was also the images that brought Robert Oakley, President Clinton's envoy, to Mogadishu to secure the release of Durant and begin the slow withdrawal from Somalia.

David knew that these events would have grave consequences for US forces for years to come. He also knew of the group called Al-Qaeda, led by Osama Bin-Laden, that would become embolden by the withdrawal of the UN and US forces from that region. The trouble was, at least for the moment, who he could get to believe in him and what he would be able to offer.

13

As 1993 ended and 1994 began, David reflected back on his present course. So far, everything was going according to his recollection of daily events. Sherry left her job to homeschool Robby and Jennifer after a run-in with the school on base at Fort Bragg. This was due to the principal's insistence that the Presidential fitness program be replaced with organized line dancing. One of the dances was called, "The Push-Tush."

David knew that it would be a career stopper to go down and slug the principal in the nose for trying to force some sort of perverted dance on a 9 year-old. After going through the school board, with a full Colonel present, without any results, David and Sherry made the decision together to homeschool.

"They acted like nothing was wrong!" Sherry spat angrily.

Robby started playing basketball at the MWR, which formed leagues for military kids. Jenny joined the gymnastic program, and David's job was as mundane as he remembered in the Executive officer position. The new Battalion commander, LTC Barrett, even had plans for him to move from Charley Company to the Battalion level as his S-1, staff administrative officer.

Everything was moving along the same way except for a few notable differences. For one, he possessed a lot more money in his current state than he ever had before. A lot more. He also knew a lot more than he ever did before, especially when it came to the knowledge of what would happen in the future. These two facts integrated into something that David was still apprehensive about and understood that this new knowledge posed certain and grave risks.

The visible elements of the larger income were displayed by more extravagant overnight hotel stays with Sherry. She also displayed beautifully, the latest expensive fashion wear that David had not seen the first time around in life. Finally, he was able to purchase two new vehicles, one of them being a 1993 Dodge minivan that Sherry insisted she still needed to haul the kids around. The other, David settled for a new 1993 Dodge Stealth, blue, 2-door ES hatchback. It looked sleek enough without appearing too elaborate for his own good and drawing undue attention on himself. He explained that he got a better deal by purchasing both vehicles as a package.

One incident took place in David's previous visit into 1993 that he wanted to avoid altogether. Remembering that he drove a new Dodge minivan to his physical training (PT) formation in the early morning hours when he pulled out in front of an Army Deuce-and-half truck that did not have its headlights working. He did not sustain any injuries, thanks to the newly equipped airbags and metal reinforcement structure of the van. The van was totaled however, and the split second he was struck, he thought that he was "toast" and would never see his family again.

David did not remember the exact day that he purchased the new van or the following day when he would have that near fatal crash. He only knew that it was in December and on a rainy morning. Whenever David would get up in the morning, if it was raining, he would make an excuse not to go to PT. A couple of times, he took a different route entirely.

Then, the day came when something unimaginable occurred and David felt sick. He heard soldiers in his unit talk about an accident that occurred one rainy morning during PT.

"Yeah, the dude was all messed up. He didn't make it."

"I heard that the Deuce didn't have its headlights on." SSG Rutherford chimed in.

"They'll get it for that!" PFC Espinosa shouted. "The guy was a Captain in the 82nd."

David walked over to the soldiers. "Are you sure the Captain didn't make it?"

"Oh, hello sir. There's no way that he could have. His head, well never mind sir. The paramedics placed a sheet over him. He was pretty messed up."

David didn't say anything. What could he say? He swallowed hard, and then walked away. Stopping briefly, he turned around to face the now silent group of soldiers. "Anyone know who he was?"

"No sir, some guy from the 82nd is what we heard."

David continued to walk away. "Some guy. Some guy who probably had a wife and kids like me." He thought.

During the next two days, David made an attempt by asking around his neighborhood and reading the Fayetteville Observer if he could find out any facts about the officer from the 82nd. He learned with little relief that the Captain was indeed from the 82nd but was not married and had no children. He lived off post in an apartment with another junior officer from the 82nd.

"At least he didn't leave behind a wife and kids," David thought to himself. The fact that the small article describing the accident mentioned that CPT Jeff Sellers was survived by his parents, a brother, and two sisters, still left David in a minor stupor for a short period of time. Would have been much longer and more severe had a wife and kids been involved.

Sherry had sensed the disturbance in David and was touched by the fact that he cared so much about a stranger. "Must be close to home since he was an airborne officer like you and crashed close to where you guys do PT."

"Yeah, a lot of our guys saw it happen." David didn't want to pursue the conversation any further. He had to move on. He would continually be alert to such matters, but he had to move on.

David, Sherry, and the kids continued with their plans to travel to Venice, Florida, where his grandmother, a widow of four years, was living. They would spend Christmas with her and enjoy the heated pool at the mobile home park and test the waters of the Gulf coast, even though David knew by experience that it would be too chilly to enjoy a good swim.

"We'll stop at Disney World," David promised "and watch the Christmas parade and fireworks!"

"Yeaaaa!" Robby and Jenny both expressed their pleasure.

Sherry smiled contently, looking forward to some time in Florida as well.

14

First Sergeant Mack stood at the rear of the tent listening to the ongoing droning of staff officers giving their evening brief to LTC Barrett. First Lieutenant Allan just completed his portion on administrative and personnel matters and walked to the rear, taking a position next to Mack.

The First Sergeant leaned over to David. "Hey sir, want to jump next Wednesday? We have some extra chutes."

David shook his head, "No thanks, top. I'm jumping next Friday when my dad's in town so he can watch."

"You can jump on both days if you want to sir."

"See if anybody needs to jump as a pay hurt."

"Yeah, I'll do that, sir."

David turned his attention to the briefing but suddenly was struck with the realization that something was terribly wrong.

"Top, cancel the jump."

"Sir? What are you talking about? We're not running it, the 82nd is. We've been given some chutes."

"Get with the ones in charge and tell them to cancel it."

"Now why would I want to do that, sir?"

"Because there will…" David stopped talking, hesitated and began again. "Just a hunch, top, that's all. I have a bad feeling about this one."

"Riiight, sir." First Sergeant Mack turned his head towards the front of the room to hear the brief. Slowly, he glanced back at David who did not know what else to say. David lowered his head.

During the staff meeting on the 23rd of March, David looked ill.

"Are you alright Lieutenant Allan?" LTC Barrett asked.

"Maybe just a touch of something, sir. I'll be okay."

"You don't look so well."

"I'll be fine, sir."

The meeting continued until Command Sergeant Major Clancy burst into the room. "There's been an accident at green ramp and there are lots of casualties!"

LTC Barrett dismissed the meeting immediately. "Let's go, Sergeant Major."

The two of them got into a waiting Humvee and sped off. David walked out of the building along with the other officers, all of whom stopped just outside the doorway to see the black, thick smoke rise from the "Green Ramp" area.

Green Ramp was the large north-south parking ramp at the west end of Pope AFB's east-west runway, used by the U.S. Army and Air Force to stage joint operations. A large open-bay building, called the pax shed, was located at Green Ramp. It was designed for numerous passengers and used for preparing troops for parachute drops. A large grassy area was just outside the building and was used for a troop staging area before drops. Behind the area, several concrete mock-ups of Air Force cargo aircraft had been constructed, where troops could rehearse their drop procedures.

David had no idea how many paratroopers were to jump that day, he couldn't remember. He would find out later that about 500 paratroopers were in the pax shed, the concrete mock-ups or resting in the grassy area. While the jumpers prepared to board several C-130s and C-141 aircraft parked on Green Ramp, the sky was filled with Air Force F-16, A-10 and C-130 aircraft conducting Air Force training. The thoughts came back to him as he headed to his office at the

Battalion. *It was a mid-air collision between an F-16 aircraft and a C-130 Hercules.*

Both aircraft were on short final approach to runway 23 at an altitude of about 300 feet when the nose of the F-16 severed the C-130's right elevator. On impact, the F-16 pilot applied full afterburner to try to recover the aircraft, but the aircraft began to disintegrate, showering debris on the runway and the surrounding area. Both F-16 crewmembers ejected, but their aircraft, still on full afterburner, continued on an arc towards Green Ramp. The F-16 struck the ground in an empty parking place between two Air Force C-130s with crews on board preparing the aircraft for departure.

When the F-16 hit the ground, its momentum carried the wreckage westward through the right wing of a C-141 parked on the ramp. The C-141 crew was also preparing the aircraft for joint Army-Air Force operations. Fortunately, no Army troops had yet boarded the plane. The wreckage of the F-16 punctured the fuel tanks in the C-141's right wing, causing a large fireball which combined with the F-16 wreckage and continued on a path taking it between Building 900 and the Pax Shed, directly into the area where the mass of Army paratroopers were sitting and standing.

Sirens wailed in the background, heading in both directions from David's nearby office. SPC Harris, his administrative assistant waited around with David. Although shaken by the events, she seemed to be holding out well. It was a somber moment.

"SPC Harris, I'm not sure how much longer LTC Barrett or the Sergeant Major will be before they return but we'll be quite busy in the next few days."

"Yes sir, I'm here if you need me for anything."

"I'm thinking some extra hours may be involved."

"Yes sir."

Around 1700 David sent SPC Harris home. "Come on in about 30 minutes earlier than usual tomorrow."

"Alright sir."

"Good-night."

"Good-night sir. See you tomorrow."

A little more than an hour later, LTC Barrett and CSM Clancy returned. David met them in the lobby, just outside the colonel's office. He didn't say anything but followed closely behind his boss.

"What a nightmarish hell that was! I never have seen anything like it before in my life!"

"Sir, are you alright?"

"Not really, David. Not really. My guess is that more than twenty soldiers lost their lives with hundreds more injured, many with burn injuries!"

David swallowed hard but remained silent.

"Some of our soldiers who were waiting to jump pulled troopers from the flames and exploding ammunition. Heroes! That's what they were. Heroes! We commandeered military and civilian vehicles to ferry the injured to Womack."

"Sounds like a real mess, sir."

"Where's SPC Harris?"

"I sent her home, sir."

"Okay, I'll need both of you here early in the morning. We're going to process a lot of awards for our heroes!"

"Yes sir, I instructed SPC Harris to come in early."

"Good. Go ahead on home. We'll start first thing in the morning."

"Yes sir."

David drove slowly home to his quarters. The junior officer housing area was not far beyond the Green ramp area where the F-16 made its final plunge.

What could I have done differently? What more could I have done?

A little over a month later, Lieutenant David Allan received word that he came up on the Captain's list for promotion. This did not surprise him, of course, not that he felt any more deserving than anybody else, but because he had already been through the routine. Family members and friends would arrive and he would actually have the rank pinned on by his Battalion Commander, wife Sherry, and kids, Robby and Jenny.

David also knew that his attempt to gain a company command back at his old PSYOP unit after having one offered to him would fall to higher powers in Washington who insisted that he attend the Officer Advanced Course first. The 6-month course, back at Fort Huachuca, Arizona, came at the same time as well, along with the predictable results of Sherry, Robby, and Jenny, all engulfed with a degree of sadness because of their departure from close friends that were made during the previous four years.

The move came in August, all within schedule, and David set out to launch his advanced studies in the military intelligence field. The house that they rented and would live in for the duration was one and the same as he remembered before. Sherry seemed a bit surprised that David led everybody straight to the house, found a great deal and moved right in, as she would tell someone later, "As if he knew it was already here."

The remainder of the year was less significant in David's eyes although he did pad his separate bank account by predicting the New York Rangers Stanley Cup victory and the outcome of the World Cup with Brazil defeating Italy. His biggest earnings however came with the bet on the cancellation of the 1994 World Series at mid-season, before the season began. Additionally, he added another big chunk of money towards his Apple Computer stock, knowing that the first release of the Macintosh Microprocessor personal computer was inevitable. Sherry still did not have any idea that David was worth so much, $1.6 million, by David's latest estimate, and growing. She did enjoy their lavish "night out" occasions and marveled at the expensive places he took her to on overnights. This was the part that David did not remember ever happening before, but he was enjoying it to the hilt. *Besides*, he reasoned, *nothing else seems to be altering the course.* David continued to play the great "officer making Captain's pay" role throughout.

During the class session when the officers had to sit through a day of lectures and briefings from the Korean "expert," David knew beforehand that he would be annoyed.

Turning to Captain Rick Larson, David said, "Listen to this guy ramble. Before he's done, he's going to say that we will be invading North Korea in 6 months. And, he tries to make it sound believable."

Rick chuckled. "He's making a strong case for it. How do you know that we don't?"

David thought for a moment. "Because he said the same thing when I was here as a Lieutenant back in '90."

"Come to think of it, I believe he said the same thing in our class too."

As before, David let it go and did not want to waste his time challenging the civilian specialist on Korea. He allowed his mind simply to wander on other things. He thought about some of the upcoming events that would be significant and what he could do, if anything, to stop them. He wasn't even sure if he really wanted to stop them in case the result would lead to something unthinkable.

After class, David pulled Rick aside. "Hey, do you remember hearing something about a FedEx Flight back in March or April 705 when there was an attempted suicidal hijacking?"

"Umm, not really, why?"

"Well, the crew managed to subdue the attacker and land at an airport and nothing happened."

"So?"

"So, this intelligence community should be taking a closer look into this and take measures to prevent future suicidal hijackers from boarding aircraft."

"Why?"

"Because, I believe that this will be the new wave of terrorism, only on passenger jets. They won't have any intention of hijacking for ransom but will try to blow the planes up with people aboard."

David purposely refrained from saying anything about commandeering planes and flying them into buildings. That will have to come later, at the right time, with the right people, and with the right information without implicating himself as a co-conspirator.

"I don't know. I doubt that this will be a trend of any kind, just some lunatic terrorist."

"Yeah, maybe you're right."

David let the subject drop, with Rick. *What could he do anyway?*

15

One of Sherry's sisters, Becky, visited the family in Arizona during the Christmas break. The day after Christmas, the five of them went on a mini-vacation trip beginning in Tombstone. They didn't spend too much time there as they continued along to the Grand Canyon. Once again, everything was the same as David remembered except for where they stayed. In keeping with a western theme, David made reservations at the Grand Hotel so that the kids could experience an authentic western atmosphere. They would stay in an executive suite, one with a balcony room featuring a desert view.

Additionally, David was told that there would be Cowboy singers and Native American dancers to entertain. "Robby and Jenny should like that," he told Sherry. "They told me that Navajo Indians would tell stories and perform some drumming and Native American singing."

David remembered a majestic view of the Canyon with the stars sparkling in the night sky. It was as if he could just reach up and grab a handful of them, they seemed so close. *I definitely want to see that sight again.* On that night that he did view the stars, the mass endless expanse, it was as he remembered. He smiled. *God, you are there, I know. You are the one who sees me!* David was taking it all in with one big inhalation after another.

"That's so beautiful," he said to Sherry.

"Yes it is, David. What a sight." She moved closer to him and held onto his arms, snuggling up against him for warmth.

David watched until the shimmering lights seemed to puzzle him. Many of the stars seemed to be fading and shining as if the heavens were sending out signals. *When did I see this before? Where was I? What was happening to me?*

Perhaps by the look on David's face, Sherry interrupted him.

"What's wrong, honey?"

"Huh, oh, nothing. Just admiring the night sky."

"You looked like you were a bit perplexed there."

"Not really. Maybe thinking too hard."

"Just enjoy the moment."

"I am, don't worry. I am. Especially with you at my side!"

Sherry smiled and tilted her head sideways onto his shoulder.

Their next stop after the Grand Canyon was to Las Vegas, Nevada. None of them had ever been there before. David had done business there, but it was indirectly and over the phone. This would be his first visit in person and with a couple of agents that he had only spoken with in the past. That part would have to wait until Sherry and her sister kept occupied with the kids.

In an effort to keep the kids distracted and otherwise occupied, David booked rooms at the "Circus Circus" Hotel. He did make one notable change in that the rooms he booked would be nothing less than one of the upper level, whirlpool suites. From this spacious room, they would also get a nice view of the city lights of Las Vegas spread across the valley.

David remembered that there was a night of trade-off when he would take the kids around the tower and play a bunch of games while Sherry and Becky toured other parts of the town. Later, they would switch off and David would be able to tour around on his own. This would be the time to meet one of his "bookies" and place some upcoming bets, such as the 1995 Super Bowl winners and yes, the strike will be resolved and there will be a 1995 season with the winner of the World Series being the Atlanta Braves over the Cleveland Indians.

"Are you sure you want to put that much down on those teams?' His agent, Steve asked him after meeting over a couple of drinks.

David just looked at him without saying a word. He didn't have to. His reputation was already a matter of discussion within Marks inner circle. "Forget I asked. I'm not sure how you do it, but you are usually dead-on. If I didn't know any better, I would think that you were from the future."

They both laughed. "Don't be ridiculous!"

The final leg of the family vacation continued to the hills east of Los Angeles and a stay with David's brother's in-laws. Danny married a blonde southern Californian girl, Laura, who he met in college. Sherry and Laura got along great together and although neither Danny nor Laura would be there, David and Sherry had met Laura's mother previously and she had extended the invite. He finally took her up on it and enjoyed a pleasant visit for a couple of days that took them into the New Year.

16

"Everyone in this room who had a CONUS assignment will be going to Korea for their next assignment!"

David knew that the moans and groans would follow the branch assignment officer's announcement from the platform in the main auditorium. Two full classes of 60 MI Branch officer's attended the brief delivered by CPT Murrell, who had traveled from Washington D.C. to line up future assignments once the Advance course was complete. In the ensuing days, CPT Murrell would meet with each of the students for 15 minutes to all but seal the deal for their next duty assignment. He would speak to each individual in alphabetical order of their last name.

One by one, most of David's classmates returned to class looking either somewhat disappointed or downright angry. CPT Ballard, who had served with David with the PSYOP Group filed past the team that David was assigned to for the exercise.

"Keith!"

Ballard stopped, and then swung around to see who was addressing him. "What's up?"

"How did it go?"

"I'm going to Korea."

"I figured. Did you try to get out of it?"

"Yeah, I told him that I couldn't go because my mother was sick and that I needed to be close by."

"Didn't work, did it?"

"Nope."

David asked a few others the same question, ones that he knew had spent time stateside on the previous three to four year tour before coming to this course. He remembered the approach that he had to take when it was his turn in order to prevent a tour to Korea, away from Sherry, Robby, and Jenny, for a year. He would do the same thing over again, expecting the same results.

David opened the door to the small classroom that was set up for CPT Murrell. Before he could close the door behind him, Murrell said, "You know you're going to Korea."

Sounding like a replay of a broken record, David knew just how to answer. "Yes, I know."

A bit surprised by his lack of an excuse not to go, CPT Murrell pointed to the empty chair at the desk to the left side of the room. A small pad of paper and a pencil rested on top.

"Go ahead and write down the places you would like to be assigned to after your Korean tour and I'll see what I can do for you."

David remembered this statement vividly and as if on cue replied back. "I'm flexible. Where are the Army's needs?"

Murrell had picked up a magazine to read and without looking at David, answered, "We always need folks at places like Fort Polk, Louisiana, Fort Bliss, Texas…" David didn't even remember the other places mentioned because he had already written down, "Fort Polk, Louisiana as his first choice and Fort Bliss, Texas as his second. He pushed his chair away from the table and handed the slip of paper to Murrell. Then, he slowly walked towards the door, waiting to hear Murrell's response that was sure to come. It did.

"You want to go to Fort Polk?"

David knew that he had to answer without enthusiasm. "Sure, if that's where the Army needs me."

"Alright, I actually need somebody there. I can probably get you there. We'll be in touch."

The news of going to Fort Polk did not sit too well with Sherry until she realized that the alternative was a year separation with David in Korea. She was sitting at a picnic table with several of the other wives while many kids played noisily in the park around them. Most of them languished bitterly as to why their husbands had to leave for Korea for a whole year without them.

Sherry tried to keep her next destination a secret until one of the wives asked, "So, what are your plans after David goes overseas?"

"Well, he's not going to Korea. We're going to Fort Polk."

"What? Fort Polk! You're going to that armpit of the world?"

"I wish we were going there instead of separating" another voice chimed in.

"Me too!"

"How did your husband manage to get a CONUS tour again?" One of the other wives asked.

"I'm not sure, really, but I'll take it."

"I would too!"

Sherry felt, imaginary or not, that the surrounding eyes around her were now out of envy and jealousy. "Robby, Jenny, come on, we have to go home now."

"I'll talk to you ladies later. I need to get some stuff done before David's parents show up next week."

"Okay, see you around."

Sherry heard a voice behind her as she headed to the minivan. "I'm going to ask Mark why the hell he didn't ask to go to Fort Polk." Other voices mumbled in agreement.

"Hurry, Robby, let's go."

"I'm trying to help Jen."

"Both of you. Just hurry up."

Four months later, the Allan's were settling into their officer quarters in the new housing section at Fort Polk. Sherry liked the house a great deal, in fact, she had mentioned to some of her family over the phone that this was the best government quarters that she has been in to date. There were surrounding parks and basketball courts dispersed throughout the long running trails that Robby and Jenny found quite appealing. There was plenty of room for Rusky to romp around as well. Robby and Jenny took turns allowing Rusky to pull them along for a ride while they wore their roller blades.

David soon discovered that the highest ranking Intelligence Officer was LTC Richardson. Richardson had been his Battalion Executive Officer when David first arrived to the 319th MI Battalion. They got along well, thanks in part to David's innovative maintenance program that he first established for the Company and then was later adopted by the whole Battalion. Shortly after arriving to Polk, LTC Richardson had the Allan's over for dinner.

Before the meal was served, David and LTC Richardson were in the den talking over some sodas. Sherry was in the kitchen helping Richardson's wife, Diane.

"I'm glad you finally made it down here. I almost had to "pull teeth" to get you here.

"Really sir, how's that?"

Your new boss, COL. Hewitt just fired his '2' and he wanted me to get him a new one, fast."

"He fired the 2?"

"Don't worry; he messed up, probably on purpose because he wanted out of the Air Defense world and COL. Hewitt wouldn't release him. Their installation security inspection failed on almost all fronts.

"Ouch!"

"Anyway, I called Branch and asked them if they had anyone they could send down here to fill a Brigade S-2 slot. Branch told me that there wasn't anyone available but that they might be able to send someone from the schoolhouse after graduation. I told them that COL. Hewitt wouldn't go for that. He wanted someone with experience. So Branch tells me, 'well, that's all we have.' I asked him who it was, maybe I'd know him. Murrell says, 'some guy named Allan.' Captain David Allan? Airborne type from Bragg? He said, 'yes sir, that's him."

David started to laugh.

"I said to Murrell, 'Send him! I have a job for him!"

"And here I am."

"Here you are. But it didn't stop there. COL. Hewitt didn't seem too pleased that you were coming from the schoolhouse without the experience he was looking for. I had to convince him that you were high-speed when you had worked for us at Bragg."

"Wow, thanks for the words, sir. Thanks for the 'string pulling' also!"

"No problem, I know you'll do well here."

"Let's eat!" Diane's voice called from the dining room.

David would have a story to share with Sherry that night. And, he would have to live up to expectations. Thinking back to that time period, he remembered what he had to do and what he needed not to do again. One of the upcoming events that started to flood his thoughts was going to take place just two months from his current time. It would happen on the 19th of April. It would not be good, at all. A bombing was going to take place in Oklahoma City at the Alfred P. Murrah Federal Building that would kill 168 people, including 8 Federal Marshals and 19 children.

In the midst of building up the 108th Air Defense Artillery Brigade's security program, David would need to gather some human intelligence on terrorists, going beyond the unchartered territory of American born terrorists. How would he be able to explain that the catastrophic event about to take place was at the hands of an all-American middle-class young man; one who served his country during Desert Storm?

David didn't know how, but he knew that he would, try to lead authorities in Timothy McVeigh and Terry Nichols direction. He had to do all of this without being implicated or tied to their scheme in some way. *But how?*

17

With his idea all laid out in writing, David drove to the Fort Polk installation Headquarters where he would find LTC Richardson. Knowing that LTC Richardson kept a full schedule, David managed to get onto his calendar through CPT Marshall, another Military Intelligence officer who worked as Richardson's aid.

"Hey, come on in and make yourself at home, CPT Allan."

"Thanks sir, I appreciate your time."

"So, what's on your mind? The 108th is treating you well from what I hear."

"Yes sir, everything is going well, thank you."

"Good to hear. So, what's up?"

Well sir, although my focus has been on ramping up the security program with the 108th, I still conduct research in the other areas."

"Good."

"I have several specialists on hand and I have assigned them to different departments. I have one of them doing research on HUMINT on his spare time and he brought something to my attention that caused me to do further research."

"Oh? What is that?"

"I've been reading a lot lately about paramilitary militia groups in the United States, such as the 'Posse Comitatus."

"The who?"

"Possee Comtatus, sir."

"I don't believe that I ever heard of them, wait, aren't they the ones who believe that the federal government is a threat to their freedom?"

"Yes sir, especially President Clinton's passage of the North American Free Trade Agreement. They believe that there exists a left-wing, globalist conspiracy that they call the New World Order."

"Interesting, CPT Allan."

"There were some members on the news not too long ago blaming the government for the FBI's 1992 shootout with Randy Weaver at Ruby Ridge."

"I see."

"They also blame the government for the 1993 siege of David Koresh and the Branch Davidians in Waco, Texas.

"What are you getting at, David? Did you find something that should concern us?"

"Well sir, not the military directly, but I believe that a couple of rogue members will plot a terrorist attack on US soil very soon."

"What makes you think that?" Do you have some specific indicators?"

David didn't say what he was thinking. Yes sir, a 100% indicator. It happened when I lived in 1995 before.

"Nothing specific, sir, just plotting some existing Intel traffic together into a matrix. Probably the most disconcerting information that I've come across indicates that a few Desert Storm veterans have been on record with anti-government talk and…"

David was cut off by Richardson's phone ringing. He saw that the Colonel looked at the blinking light and reached for the receiver. "Excuse me, David, but I need to take this."

Sensing that LTC Richardson was only slightly interested in his findings, David got up to leave. LTC Richardson nodded his approval and then David heard him speak into the mouthpiece. "Just a minute. David, keep up your search and let me know if you come across anything concrete that we might be able to present."

"Roger that, sir."

David left the building wondering what his next step would be. *Should I make an anonymous call to the FBI?* He went back to his office to continue his research; trying to find something that would tie Timothy McVeigh, Terry Nichols, and Michael Fortier, to their basic training connection at Fort Benning, Georgia in 1988. None of his specialists were really looking into the matter at all, so he was on his own. And, whatever he did, he could not reveal anything that would implicate his foreknowledge.

Time was running out but he found something that he could confront LTC Richardson with. At the risk of becoming an annoying nuisance to the officer who helped him remain stateside, he called his office. After several, "He'll get back with you's" from CPT Marshall LTC Richardson finally returned his call.

"What did you find, David?"

"Sir, do you remember a couple of years ago, in '93, when the Alfred P. Murrah Federal Building in Oklahoma City was targeted by the white supremacist group called, 'The Covenant, The Sword, and the Arm of the Lord?"

"Maybe vaguely."

"They plotted to park a vehicle in front of the Federal Building and blow it up with rockets detonated by a timer."

"Okay, David. You could be onto something there. Go on."

"Well sir, a militia group could be planning another attack similar to that one during the Waco anniversary or something."

"Hmmm, interesting thought. I'll need some more information. I'll tell you what, put together an INTSUM about your findings on American militia groups and I'll look at it when you're finished. No guarantees, but if it sounds convincing enough, I might be able to get a couple of the right guys in DC to look further into it."

"Thank you, sir. I appreciate this."

"David, if you're right about a terrorist bomb here set off by our own, God help us."

"Yes sir."

April 19th was less than a week away. Anytime David questioned LTC Richardson about the INTSUM report that he had submitted, LTC Richardson's answer was the same. "I haven't had time to look at it closely."

With time running out, LTC Richardson finally read through it but the information did not seem conclusive enough for him to send to a higher level. "This is a good report David, but it lacks any kind of evidence. It's mostly speculatively stated."

David already knew this would be true. How else could he reveal information without coming out and say, *Listen, I'm from the future!*

David though of one more idea but there was only three days before the catastrophic event would take place. *Why hadn't I thought of this before?*

It took him a while to find the phone number after an extensive search, but once he did, David drove down to Lake Charles, pulled into a gas station and dialed the number.

"Hello, this is William Fielder."

"Bill, this is David Allan. Do you remember me?"

"David, of course. How could I ever forget you?"

"I was hoping you would say something like that."

"It's been a long time. How is the army treating you these days?

"It's going well so far. I'm still working intelligence, this time with an ADA unit."

"I see. Good for you. What can I do for you? This must be important."

"It is. I was doing some research with my current unit and I came across something that may be in your domain." David went on to explain everything that he had already spoke with LTC Richardson about but now the information was passed along to a different agency, the FBI.

"Thanks for letting me know this, David. Actually, this sort of thing is being tracked and we have a pretty good surveillance net over such groups."

David, once again refrained from saying, *maybe so, but you don't have a clue about Timothy McVeigh, Terry Nichols, or Michael Fortier.* The fact was, he couldn't find any information about them anywhere.

He wanted to close with, Okay Bill, just be sure that all of your federal offices take extra precautions on the 19th of April or, don't forget, the Branch Davidians Waco disaster has an anniversary coming up on the 19th.

Instead, he just closed with, "Well, I just wanted to let you know what I stumbled across here but it sounds like you have it all covered."

"Thanks for calling David. Always good to hear from you."

David woke up feeling sick to his stomach on the morning of the 19th.

"I don't feel so well, Sherry. Maybe I'll go in to sick call and get some free meds.

"You don't look well, David. Why don't you just stay in bed; I'll call your office and…"

"You know it doesn't work that way, dear. I'll be alright."

Sherry just looked at him, knowing that to argue would be a waste of time.

David drove by the office and told his senior enlisted officer, Sergeant Major Cox, that he had to take care of some business and that he should be back by noon.

"Got you covered, sir."

The drive to Lake Charles took about 90 minutes. David went to the south side of town to locate a remote gas station; one with a phone booth. He finally found one that suited his purpose. Walking into the booth after making sure that there were no people in sight, he slipped on a pair of surgeon's gloves and dialed a number that he pulled from his pocket.

There was no answer on the other end. *Jesus!*

David tried again and kept letting the phone ring. Still no answer. He hung up, looked around, noted a car pulling into the station and quickly got back into his car. The man in his late thirties, dressed in a white t-shirt and jeans glanced quickly in his direction but didn't seem to notice David sitting low, trying not to be seen.

Then David waited. Finally, the customer ran out, jumped into his car and peeled away with his tires screeching against the pavement. David's heart sank. *Did that guy just rob the place? That would be all I need.* Nothing happened. No storeowner running out yelling, "I've just been robbed!" Nobody staggering out with their hand clutched to their chest; nothing. David breathed a sigh of relief.

Returning to the booth, he dialed the number on the torn piece of paper again. This time, somebody answered on the other end.

"Front desk, Murrah Federal Building. Can I help you?'

David had to play this with wisdom and tact. "Yes, I was wondering, do you happen to notice if there is a yellow Ryder truck parked out front of your building on the eastern end?"

"I can't see from here, why? Who is this?"

"Could you check it out?'

"Listen, I don't have time. Why don't you…" Just then David heard someone pull into the parking lot and didn't hear the voice on the other end. He also didn't hear that there was a clicking sound followed by a dial tone.

Two men got out of a pick-up truck and went inside.

"Dear God!" David fished for more coins to drop into the slot.

Then he dialed the number again. The phone rang. In fact, it rang several times. Nobody picked it up on the other end.

He left it ringing. *I knew I should have called much sooner!*

The two men emerged from the storefront with a couple of sodas and a pack of cigarettes. Both stopped long enough to check out the uniformed figure inside the phone booth. David watched them until they got into the truck and drove off.

"Hello! Hello!"

David quickly held the phone back to his ear. "Yes, sorry. I…"

"It's you again! Who is this?"

"It doesn't matter. Listen. I don't have time. Don't hang up, please! Is there a Ryder truck…?"

"YOU LISTEN, Mister! I don't know who you think you are but I'm gonna track you down and lock your ass up…!

"EVACUATE! NOW!" David finally blurted.

"THAT's IT! I'm running a tracer on you right now buster!"

David hung up quickly. There he stood, gloved hand still on the phone. Sweat dripping down his face. His heart pounding. "Oh God, why?' he cried. The tears flowed. He got back into his car and sat there with his head down on the steering wheel. A wrap on his window caused him to jump.

"You alright, sir?" The heavy accented Cajun voice came from a man who looked to be in his late forties. This oval faced guy with thinning hair wore glasses and he seemed genuinely concerned.

"I'm fine, thanks." David reached for his keys in the ignition.

"You don't look so good!"

"What? I'm fine!"

The man slowly walked away. "Drive careful now."

"Okay, thanks.

David said a quick prayer and called Bill Fielder's number, praying and sweating the whole time that he would answer.

"Fielder!"

"Thank God!"

"Hello?"

"Bill, it's me, David Allan."

"Hi David, whatever I can do for you, make it quick. I'm running late for a meeting. You were lucky to catch me because I just returned back to the office to retrieve a folder when the phone rang."

"Bill, I don't know how to say this, but do you remember that conversation we had a week ago about the home-grown militia groups?"

"Yes, in fact that is what our meeting is going to cover."

"Listen to me carefully, please. There is little time and I cannot explain where I got this information but please, I beg you, call your contacts at the Alfred P. Murrah Federal Building in Oklahoma City now! Ask them to look for a yellow Ryder truck parked outside the building, and hurry! There isn't much time!"

Bill listened silently, stunned by what he was hearing. "David, I will make the call. Stay on this line."

"Okay, please hurry."

The phone rang on the desk of Brad Grant. "Hello, this is Grant."

"Grant, Fielder here from the Tampa office."

"Oh, hey, how…" Brad was cut off.

"No time. Listen, can you get some folks to look outside your building for a yellow Ryder truck?"

"Sure Bill, what's this…?"

"No time, now!"

"Give me a minute."

David waited what seemed like an eternity. *Come on, come on*!

"Bill, there is one parked out front. I have a guy going down there now to have the driver move it."

"No! Evacuate the building immediately!"

Brad was speechless. "Bill?"

"Immediately! And keep me posted!"

Brad set the fire alarm off and began the emergency evacuation procedures for his staff in the building. Fortunately, the alarm system registered throughout the building. Most of the building's occupants thought that it was simply a drill and ignored the alarm. Brad had his team move quickly throughout the building to attempt directing everybody out the back side away from the truck.

Day care workers were busily herding children towards the front of the building when one of Brad's men stopped them and directed them to the back. When they filed outside, they were joined by others piling out the back entrance as well.

Brad was on a Walkie talkie when a blast suddenly ripped through atmosphere sending shock waves reverberating through the building. He, along with everyone else were thrown to the ground. Glass shattered and rained down all around the building.

"MY, GOD!"

Brad stood up shakily, holding his head. Everyone around him in the grassy area behind the building seemed to fine except for the shock. Kids were screaming and crying while many ran to their aid to help keep them calm. Brad went immediately into operation mode and began setting up security perimeters, account for his people, and call in reinforcements.

The Emergency Medical Services Authority were already headed to the scene, having heard the blast. The people nearby taking care of their own business also witnessed or heard the blast and began arriving to assist the victims and emergency workers. The EMS command post was set up almost immediate following the attack and oversaw triage, treatment, transportation, and decontamination. Within 23 minutes of the bombing, the State Emergency Operations Center (SEOC) was set up, consisting of representatives from the state departments of public safety, human services, military, health, and education.

"David. Did you hear what happened?" Bill asked.

"Tell me you got everybody out of the building, Bill."

"Most everybody. Reports are still coming in but looks like there were 70 casualties overall, about 12 of them dead."

"Any children, Bill?"

Bill thought for a moment. "How did you know there were children there? It doesn't matter now, we'll talk soon. No reports of any children casualties."

"Thank God!"

"You know that we need to talk about this. Soon!"

"I know Bill and I'll try to explain everything."

"Alright, I'll be in touch. And David?"

"Yes?"

"Thank you."

David did not know how to answer. "I'm looking forward to seeing you soon, Bill."

"Me too. You better believe it!"

David headed back north to Fort Polk. He left the radio off. He was already relieved about the news that by now had reached the airwaves across the continent. A lonesome loser named Timothy McVeigh; a Gulf War veteran; behind the grisly massacre of detonating an explosive-filled Ryder truck parked in front of the Alfred P. Murrah Federal Building in Oklahoma City.

David tried to think how many lives were lost before he went back in time, when he lived this life previously. The numbers were coming to his mind slowly. *Wasn't it around 168 lives lost, 19 of them children, and more than 600 injured?* David couldn't remember the exact numbers.

Within 90 minutes of the explosion, Timothy McVeigh was stopped as he was traveling north on Interstate 35 near Perry, Oklahoma by an Oklahoma

State Trooper. McVeigh was charged with driving without a license plate and arrested for unlawfully carrying a weapon. Forensic evidence quickly linked McVeigh and Terry Nichols to the attack; Nichols was arrested, and within days both were charged.

Maybe if David had remembered the details prior to the bombing, he could have stopped it altogether. If only he could have remembered that McVeigh and Nichols held their bags of high-grade ammonium nitrate fertilizer, 55-gallon drums of liquid nitro methane, and several crates of explosive Tovex, the whole thing could have been prevented. But David did not remember those facts. He could only recall the date of the explosion because of the anniversary of the Waco attack and that was due largely in part to the media coverage of the event.

18

The phone on David's desk rang for the third time before he decided to pick it up. He was still feeling a bit dazed by the Oklahoma City bombing, wondering what, if anything, he could have done differently to prevent the (in his mind) re-occurrence.

"Hello, Brigade S-2, this is Captain Allan, can I help you?

"Hello, David. This is Bill, from Tampa."

"Bill, hello. How are you?"

"Okay, considering. Can we talk in private?"

"Ah, sure. Are you here in Louisiana?"

"Yes, I am. How about we meet at the Catfish junction for lunch today, say around noon? Are you free?"

"Yes. I'll be there."

"Good, thanks. Looking forward to seeing you again."

"Yes, likewise. It's been a while.

David set the phone down easily, held it a few seconds and then dialed the number to his quarters to call Sherry.

"Hello?"

"Hey honey, I won't be home for lunch today. Got to do something official."

"Alright. We'll eat without you. The kids will just have to miss their PT."

"I'll cover that when I get home after work."

"Okay, sounds good. I love you."

"Love you too, babe."

Since moving from Fort Bragg to Fort Huachuca and then to Fort Polk, all in a 6-month period, Sherry decided to homeschool Robby and Jenny. Their Physical Education was accomplished during the lunch hours when David came home and gave them some physical training, the military terminology for exercising.

David spotted Bill sitting at a small table in the far end of the room with his back to the wall and facing the door. He wore a white buttoned dress shirt and navy trousers. The white-haired man was in his mid-sixties and he sported a well-groomed moustache.

Bill slid his chair smoothly behind him and stood waiting as David approached his table. At six foot, two inches, Bill was slim and in good condition. David thought back at the time Bill drove home a lesson in tennis 8 years before. It was ugly, the score being 6-0, 6-0. All David remembered was chasing after tennis balls all day in the hot Tampa sun without having a chance to hit the ball back.

"Great to see you again." Bill extended his hand and David was prepared for his firm grip.

"Good seeing you, sir. David countered.

"Since when did you start calling me sir?"

"I don't know. Sorry, Bill."

"That's better. Let's get something to eat, just like old times. Then, I'd like to discuss something with you."

"Sounds good. I can pick up the tab this time," David volunteered, "unlike the past."

Bill chuckled. "That won't be necessary. I arranged the meeting. But, I appreciate the offer."

David could only surmise that the meeting had to do with his knowledge about the Oklahoma City bombing. David ordered his favorite dish of the large plate of crawfish while Bill settled for the Crawfish et'tufe. Small talk ensued while they devoured their meal.

"So that was the last time you ever saw the Russian? That doesn't surprise me. They left in a hurry after the wall fell."

"The Army guys tried to re-establish contact for a few more years but then called it off for good, about two years ago."

The blond waitress, looking like she was in her late teens or early twenties stopped at their table. "Can I get you gentlemen anything else?"

"No, we're fine for now," Bill answered quickly.

David was surprised that Bill understood her Cajun accent. They waited for her to leave before Bill began. "David, the reason I wanted to meet with you and have this talk is because of the Oklahoma City incident."

"I thought that it might be."

"You knew this was going to happen, didn't you?"

"What makes you think that I would…"

"Don't worry, David. I don't for a minute believe that you had anything to do with this. But, you knew this was going to happen, right?"

David was speechless.

David, I went to Walter Reed and was able to get into your medical record."

"How did…?" David was interrupted for the second time.

"Not that it matters right now, but I read Dr. Meyers report and his assessment about you."

"I don't know what his assessment was, actually, other than he told me that I would be okay and that I should stay up to date with my check-ups."

Bill just looked at him. "Did you tell Dr. Meyers a story about being in a place called Balad, Iraq in 2003 as a Major? That you helped in the capture of Saddam Hussein?"

David felt edgy, and could feel his heart thump through his chest. *God, I forgot about that!* "I don't recall. Was that in the report?"

Bill took a sip from his red plastic glass, and then set it down. "I can help you David, but this is not the time to play games or to have memory lapse."

David knew that his 'gig' was up. If there was anybody he could trust, outside of Sherry, it was Bill. "Okay, I wasn't sure if I had been dreaming at first but after I started picking winners in sporting events and certain world events materialized as I remembered them, I knew it couldn't be a dream. It isn't is it?"

"I came across your account also, David. I'm not too concerned about that right now."

"But you are concerned about?"

"Do the guys you worked with from the 902nd know about your theory with the American militia and Oklahoma City?"

"No, I did not contact them."

"Good. Who else did you tell?"

"I mentioned something about the American militias to LTC Richardson, but I put it in an IntSum so that I would not draw attention to myself.

"You probably have his attention more so now."

"Yes, as a matter of fact, he did call me to his office after the bombing."

"What did he say?"

"Just that this whole thing was unbelievable and that maybe he should have listened to me about pursuing my findings."

"Let's hope that's all he's thinking and hasn't moved up the chain with your predictive analysis."

"Why?" David was curious now.

"David, I think highly of you and your family. Have you ever read the book, 'Repeat,' by Ken Grimwood?"

"No, I can't say that I have. Never even heard of him."

"I brought you a copy. It was written in 1988, about the time we were meeting in Florida. I want you to pay particular attention to chapters 16 and 17. Here, take a look.

Bill reached down to his leather portfolio case and pulled out a red and white book with a picture of a man's face divided into several sections.

"Why, what's this all about?"

"Just read it. It has to do with the phenomenon that you are going through right now. I'll stay in touch. I'm somewhat in the neighborhood for a few days, New Orleans, actually. Do you think you could get away for a couple of days and come down to New Orleans? You could even bring Sherry and the kids. I'll put you up in a nice place. Of course, she cannot know anything about this either."

"Sounds like fun but what do I tell her?"

Just tell her that you need to talk with me for a couple of days about the Russian business. Tell her that I'm writing a memoir and I wanted to get some firsthand information from you and that as an incentive, I arranged a weekend for the whole family."

'I believe that would work! I'll talk with her tonight!"

"Just remember to keep tight lipped about this other business."

"No problem there."

"Meanwhile, read the book. Pay close attention to those chapters, will you? I don't want you to end up in the same predicament.

"Now you really have my curiosity."

"We'll talk in New Orleans. You have some fast reading to do. I cannot move forward until we discuss your feelings about what you read."

"Okay, Bill. Thanks for this. What's next?"

"Just read the book. We'll talk. It's imperative that when we meet the next time, you will have this completed."

19

Tampa, Florida; August, 2001

Bill Fielder sat in his office in Tampa reviewing a number of CIA documents that needed to be correlated and processed for release to the local FBI. A data cruncher sitting somewhere in the dark reading unrelated documents had highlighted a name on a report. He was convinced after his meeting in New Orleans with David that something catastrophic would happen soon. David told him that horrific terrorists' events would take place in the year 2001. Although the full details were a bit sketchy at the time, David would call and provide a little more information, little-by-little as he recalled them. Bill was satisfied at the moment but time was running out.

It had been six years since he talked with David in New Orleans. David had advanced in his career to a Major in the Acquisition Corps after a successful command at McGregor Range, just north of Fort Bliss, Texas in El Paso. He guarded the information that David gave him with the utmost secrecy, filing it away under, *Top Secret*.

"Mohamed Atta as-Sayyid!" This name caught Bill's attention as he sifted through David's notes because although he lived in the US on a tourist/ business visa, he had his driver's license revoked in

absentia after he failed to show up in traffic court. Normally, this would not have caught anybody's attention. But something about the name bothered Bill. He heard it before somewhere, but where? It was familiar.

Finally, the name "rang a bell." His big dilemma was what to do with the ringing in his head. The Israeli Mossad had passed on some information that included Atta along with 18 others in a report on Middle Eastern operatives. All were known to have been involved with the Hamburg Islamic Jihad Cell in one manner or another. The question was how to get this information into the hands of the right people to take appropriate action without revealing the source and without scaring off the terrorist.

Technically the CIA had no authority to operate in the USA as they were empowered to gather intelligence outside the US. It was the FBI's job to handle domestic terror. *This could be one of those typical inter-agency fiascos,* Bill thought to himself. The better idea was to take charge within the FBI department and keep it within the agency. This would require careful planning.

Protocol required him to write up a report and pass it up to his Station Chief who would determine who in the FBI to transfer it to. More paperwork. It could also jeopardize David's position, if not his life and that of his family's. Bill would submit a generic report on domestic terrorism and would make sure that the Mossad report was included. He would bring up the names David remembered about Middle Eastern terrorists planning an attack for the 11th of September, 2001.

Seattle, Washington: September 10, 2001

David's jet winged its way westward towards Ft. Lewis in the state of Washington. David was on his way to conduct meetings with some of the commanders and operations officers about the newly fielded Stryker vehicles, which would soon make their way to Ft. Polk and take part in high profile exercises. It was one of David's responsibilities to ensure that the new instrumentation system being installed at the JRTC would be sufficient to communicate with the Stryker vehicles conducting their exercises.

The vehicles were to be fitted with the EPLARS (Enhanced Precision Locating and Reporting System) and FBCB2 (Force XXI Battle Command, Brigade-and-Below), which provides the situational awareness and command and control to the lowest tactical echelons, or quite simply, the troops who are on the ground. It was David's project to ensure a seamless facilitation between the flow of battle on the ground to interoperate with the main Instrumentation systems at the JRTC.

He was looking forward to the trip because he had never been to the Pacific Northwest before and he recently discovered that one of his old Special Forces buddies, Steve Jorgensen, just retired from the Army and was working at the Army hospital there. "I'm going to make a point of seeing him." He told Sherry.

His flight was uneventful and David thought how spectacular Mount Rainer looked in the clear blue sky as he watched it pass on the left side of the aircraft.

Portland, Maine: September 11, 2001

Atta did not sleep much the night before. He was not sure if it was the late night pizza he and Abdulaziz al-Omari had eaten or the excitement of the execution of their operation and immortal wedding to follow. He had bathed and purified himself and then had meticulously dressed. His dark slacks and powder blue shirt were pressed. A leather bag containing a few items was packed. Into the bag he slipped his will and a message written in Arabic the night before:

"Make an oath to die and renew your intentions. You should feel complete tranquility, because the time between you and your marriage in heaven is very short. Check your weapon before you leave and long before you leave. You must make your knife sharp and you must not discomfort your animal during the slaughter."

Atta, the ringleader of the attacks, and a fellow hijacker, al-Omari, arrived at the Portland Maine airport at 05:41 Eastern Daylight Time. Then they boarded Colgan Air Flight 5930 and flew to Boston, arriving at Logan at 06:45. Both men had first class tickets with a connecting flight to Los Angeles. Three other men arrived to Logan around the same time in a rental car. Their names were, Waleed al-Shehri, Wail al-Shehri, and Satam al-Suqami.

At 06:52, Marwan al-Shehhi, another person of interest made a call from a pay phone in Logan Airport to Atta's cell phone. "Yes?" Atta asked answering the phone.

"It is a wonderful day to get married, is it not?" Marwan asked wanting to confirm that the operation was indeed on.

"A wonderful day indeed. I will see you at the wedding where we will rejoice together!" Atta replied.

"I will see you there, my brother." Marwan confirmed as the phone hung up.

Suqami, Wail al-Shehri, and Waleed al-Shehri checked in for the flight in Boston. By 07:10, all five men were waiting at Gate B32 to board flight 11.

The flight attendant behind the desk nervously picked up the microphone and announced, "Ladies and gentlemen, due to some minor maintenance issues, the aircraft will be delayed by 30 minutes. We apologize for any inconvenience but we should be able to board in 30 minutes."

The five men exchanged glances but said nothing. Al-Shehhi got up to pace around the floor with Atta's eyes on him but no words were exchanged. There were a few groans from other passengers but most resumed their current position except for a couple who went to the desk to get further details.

Not long afterwards, the aircraft, a Boeing 767-223ER, slowly rolled up to the terminal. Most of the passengers gathered their belongings and started to make their way towards the door leading to the aircraft.

The flight attendant lifted the microphone and once again seemed a little more nervous than usual. She was flanked by two males, each wearing a white button shirt with an American Airline logo above their pockets.

"Ladies and gentlemen, we apologize for the delay but we are now ready to board first class passengers and only first class at this time."

There were a few more complaints as those who had first class tickets moved to the front of the line.

Then, as the two American Airline officials took their positions to take the tickets, the passengers inched their way forward.

"Mr. and Mrs. Angelokas, could I ask you two to step over here for a brief moment?"

The couple looked confused and irritated. "What's this all about?" Mr. Angell asked.

"No problems, just routine random checks."

Seeing that there were two men immediately behind them looking perturbed, they reluctantly followed a third man in a security uniform who led them behind a partition.

The next men move forward. The agent took their tickets and said, "Have a nice flight Mr. Atta. Have a nice flight Mr. Omari."

Neither of them responded.

About five others were also selected to move behind the partition, including Dan Levin while Suqami, Waleed and Wail were let through to the plane. Once the five of them had entered the aircraft, the ticket agent shut the door to the confused indignation of the rest of the passengers.

"What the hell is going on?" One of them yelled.

The American airline agents were joined with four others and a small security team of three men. "Please, ladies and gentlemen, please. Can we have you please be seated for just a moment, please!"

As the officials and security team helped dissolve any potential confrontation, the passengers began to take seats, all appearing on the edge. On another side of Logan airport in the United Airlines section, a similar scenario was taking place.

Mohamed Atta sat in business class seat 8D with Abdulaziz al-Omari in 8G and Suqami in 10B. Waleed al-Shehri and Wail al-Shehri sat in first class seats 2B and 2A. After realizing that no more passengers were boarding the aircraft, Atta became alarmed. "Where are the other passengers? Where are the attendants?" Atta yelled in Arabic.

Before anyone could answer, a group of black-clad soldiers erupted from the coach section which had been curtained off and two more burst upon the scene, one from the cockpit and the other from the front lavatory.

"Allah Akbar!" Al-Omari screamed as he leaped from his seat welding a knife. He was promptly shot twice, once in the heart and the other on the forehead.

The other four men were motionless, shocked expressions on their faces. The lead soldier from the front yelled for everybody to lift their hands high where they could be seen. His command was repeated in Arabic by another soldier.

Atta reached down towards his belt and was swiftly struck on the head with an assault rifle butt, knocking him cold. The other three men were handled sternly and cuffed by other soldiers. Within minutes, one terrorist lay dead, another wounded, and three subdued with handcuffs and a hood placed over their heads.

The plane slowly began moving away from the terminal and moved out of sight into a nearby hangar. Ten minutes later, a United Airline, Flight 175, another Los Angeles–bound Boeing 767, entered the same hangar. Inside the aircraft, another five men were ushered out of the plane, all in handcuffs and wearing a hood over their heads. Together, eight men were led into a waiting oversized van with no back windows or markings of any kind. Another, Atta, was wheeled into a waiting ambulance, also without markings, and he was joined by Omari, who was zipped into a body bag and placed onto a stretcher.

One of the lead soldiers was on the phone with a connection to Washington. The downtown office was filled with FBI agents, screens, phones, and various other electronic devices used for monitoring and communication purposes. The 6 foot 3 inch agent, wearing a light blue button shirt with his sleeves rolled back to his elbow turned to Bill Fielder and lifted his fist high with the thumbs up.

Bill turned to Pete Colson and smiled. "Thank God. But we still have two more that we know of."

"We're tracking them now." Pete answered.

The room was still bustling with activity as agents moved with a purpose to their assigned positions at the Emergency Operation Center (EOC). The director of the FBI had just finished speaking on the hotline to the president. Bill walked closer to hear the conversation.

"Yes sir, two aircraft have been confirmed as a take down by our side. They are all in custody."

"No sir, no American casualties."

"Yes sir, we believe there are two more aircraft at least."

"No sir, we don't know who is responsible at this time but we intend to find out."

"Yes sir, we'll stay on it and keep you informed of the situation as it develops.

"Thank you sir. Yes, okay. Thank you."

Looking at Bill after hanging up, the director asked, "What do we have?"

"Still tracking it." Bill replied.

American Airlines Flight 77 was preparing for a flight to Los Angeles from Dulles International airport just outside of Washington D.C. Like the two aircraft in Boston, the Boeing 757-223 was attempting its daily scheduled morning transcontinental service when the specially trained anti-terrorist FBI team stormed the plane as it sat on the tarmac waiting for the remaining passengers to load after the first class passengers entered. One of the men captured, Hani Hanjour, was trained as a pilot.

Bill was a bit worried about the fourth aircraft because David's information was sketchier. Additionally, David was not aware of any other aircraft beyond the United Airlines flight from Newark International Airport in Newark, New Jersey, to San Francisco International Airport in San Francisco, California. Bill was able to trace such a flight scheduled as Flight 93. Like the other three counter-terrorist actions, the fourth was also successful in similar fashion.

Bill listened to the director on the phone to the president again.

"Yes sir, we believe that we stopped all of the attacks although our agency in coordination with local law enforcement and airline executives have been told to stop and report any groups of three or more Arabic males trying to board an aircraft."

"Yes sir, we hope so."

Ft. Lewis, Washington: September 11, 2001

The phone alongside David's bed rang again dragging him out of a restless sleep. He had actually awakened over three hours earlier at 6 am Eastern Time as his body was tuned to early rising. But it was not fun getting up at 3 AM in a hotel room 3000 miles away from home so David had rolled over and had fallen back into a shallow sleep. He answered the phone, heard the recording and the time, 5:45 AM, and then sat up in bed. Time to begin his daily routine. The hotel had a small coffee percolator in the room with all the fixings he needed to brew his morning cup of Java. Setting that process in motion he opened his suitcase and pulled out the travel valise with his razor and toothbrush. It was time to take his morning shower and prepare for the day. The first thing he did was to flip on the television to any kind of news he could find. At the moment, only local stuff was being reported. He decided that he would have time to take a shower before hearing anything in the news about what he remembered was a tragic day in his previous life. *Previous life?* David still shuttered at the thought.

When he was finished, he heard the up-tempo voices of national news anchors on the TV set. David frantically scurried to the television. What he saw amazed him. It was indeed an incredible sight! There was a shot of both the World Trade Centers in New York City...still standing and without smoke. David sat down on the edge of his bed and stared in disbelief. David listened closely as various news reports poured in from all the channels that he surfed through.

David finally stopped on one of the stations, he wasn't sure which one but a picture of the Pentagon caught his attention.

"We just got word that one of the most horrific terrorist plots against our nation has been foiled that would have had passenger airliners crash through both Trade Centers in New York, the Pentagon, and the Capitol!"

"Wait, did you say that terrorists were going to crash aircraft into these buildings? That's unbelievable!"

"Yes, Mike, from what we have been able to ascertain at the moment..."

David let the words fade as he watched the screen and saw that the New York Trade Centers along with the Pentagon were all still standing without any trace of the horrific vision he thought he remembered during a different time. *Maybe even a different place?* David didn't know for sure.

Hamburg, Germany

Hassan watched in horror as the reports filtered through all the news channels about how a massive terrorist plot had been discovered and stopped in America. "Something happened to Mohammed." Hassan hissed.

Hassan knew that each tower had been designed with a central core of columns in which the elevators were encased. The perimeter of the building had columns rising vertically from floor to floor. Each floor's structure was supported by the floor above it. The planes impact had to have destroyed numerous columns both on the exterior and at the core.

"The plan was perfect. What went wrong?"

Had the plan been fulfilled, Hassan was aware that by his analysis the towers would have fallen in time because of the duo dynamic forces of energy at play. One was the dynamic release of energy upon impact; hundreds of millions of pounds of energy released. The aviation fuel had two components; a dynamic and kinetic or stored energy. The weight of the fuel and its velocity were dynamic and released upon impact.

This would have caused the instantaneous destruction of the columns. But the fuel is aviation fuel; it does not explode but rather burns therefore it releases its kinetic or stored energy over time in the form of heat; in this case, tremendous heat. Continuous flames generating heat that cooks concrete causing it to weaken and crack while simultaneously raising the temperature of the steel structure ever so slowly until the steel reaches the point where it softens and bends unable to sustain the load it carries.

The impact of the planes would have taken out two or three floors of the building. The heat did the rest. The structure would no longer support the weight above it and the upper floors collapsed downward. Columns are able to withstand incredible vertical loads but are not so good at loads pulling from the sides. As the upper floors collapsed downward the load was no longer stacked one floor on top of the other. Suddenly all the weight of the upper floors would fall downward through the center of the building pulling the columns inward. Once it began the process could not be stopped. Both towers would have been doomed from the point of impact. His concept, the plan he had proposed to Atta years earlier had gone wrong. *What went wrong?*

20

"David. The agency cannot ever thank you enough." Bill said as they sat at a café in Clearwater, Florida. "This is just a little something to show our gratitude."

Bill handed David an envelope as they sipped drinks and watched the beach activity. "This isn't necessary, Bill."

"It's nothing, just take Sherry away from here for a while and enjoy some time off. Besides, I'm late giving you anything for your 20th anniversary."

David smiled. "Thanks Bill, I really appreciate it."

"Anytime!"

"So, what is the government response to the Al-Qaeda plot?" David asked.

Bill chuckled. "The big guy was really pissed about the whole thing. He put Rumsfeld on the task to do something and the only thing they could think of at the time was to bomb the smithereens out of Afghanistan."

"That always works," David said sarcastically.

"But then, some Special Forces Major from 5th Group went to CENTCOM and talked sense with the conventional stars. He convinced somebody that sending ODA Special Forces teams in to link up with Afghan rebels who fought the Soviets was a brilliant idea."

"Sounds good to me."

"Well, it's working. An ODA team linked up with a former leader named Karzai in the south and other teams linked up with some Afghan generals in the north, and there are great strides being made against the Taliban and Al-Qaeda."

"Any luck getting Bin-Laden?"

"Not yet, but it's just a matter of time. Our guys are fighting with some experienced Afghan soldiers who are on our side, that is, at least for the moment."

David chuckled, remembering his conversation with the KGB agent in the '80s.

Bill continued. Yeah, I don't know if you ever heard of them before but the Afghan generals include Dostum, Noor, and Mohaqeq, all good leaders."

The names did not register with David.

"Anyway, I need to go. Great talking to you, and thanks again, David. Really."

They both stood, shook hands, and then Bill sauntered over to his car and then drove off as the sun was beginning to set. David sat back down and opened the envelop. Inside were two tickets for a one week Caribbean cruise to St. Maarten, Antigua, St. Lucia, and Barbados!

21

Spotting an empty lounge chair on the beachfront, a pretty young lady with sandy-colored hair escaping from beneath a straw, sauntered over and sat next to David. Startled, he made a quick glance to see if Sherry was anywhere near and then heard the girl say, "I hope you don't mind me sitting here just for a brief moment. The other lady that was just here, your wife I presume, seems like she will be waiting a while for her order so I thought I come by to say hi."

David looked at her a moment. "Wait, don't I know you?"

"Maybe we have met at another time." She answered. There was a moment of silence. David could see that she was conspicuously trying to keep her eyes behind her sunglasses. Suddenly, Déjà vu engulfed David's entire being. Although breathing harder and sitting up, he waited for the next question, nonetheless.

"You are...!" He was interrupted.

"Sir, can I ask you something?"

"You can!" He answered, almost too quickly. "But you already know how I'm going to answer, don't you?"

She chuckled. "You're right, sir. I don't need to ask you the same question and you don't need to reply with the same answer."

Both were silent for a few seconds. "You probably don't even need to be calling me sir, because, aren't you, like some sort of guardian angel?" David asked.

Again, the reassuring smile. She did not answer.

David was startled. His emotions mixed with fascination, fear, excitement; all at once. One thing for sure, he didn't know what to say next.

"So, you had it all to do over again and you did it!" She said.

David was speechless.

"Things will be different now, not as you once knew them to be. I have something to give you, a symbolic pillar to measure your time. You had it before but misplaced it in the Iraqi desert."

"Wait a minute, so I was there..." Again, the girl interrupted David.

"The emerald eye inside what you call a marble is alive and represents the color of your wife's eyes. She is the one who has been chosen for you to share this life."

The girl gave David the marble as he remained stunned. He didn't have the words.

"You may also remember me as Michal Gabriel. Keep the marble and never let it go."

She stood to go and extended her hand. "Sir, it's been a pleasure. I need to go now."

Then she turned around and walked towards the crystal blue sea. David watched her until she waded further away until he lost sight of her.

Wait! That can't be a good thing! David thought. He continued to scan the two-toned blue horizon but only saw water. At that moment, Sherry returned with two drinks in her hand.

"What's wrong, honey, you looked like you've seen a ghost?"

"Maybe I did." David replied. Excuse me for just a minute. Okay?"

"Uh, sure, where are…?"

David had already jumped out of his chair and ran towards the sinking sea. He swam as hard as he could towards the spot where he last saw Michal, stopping for air and looking for any sign of a struggle every few seconds. The current seemed to becoming stronger, yanking him below the surface more often than he would have liked. In the background, he heard people yelling. He thought that he heard Sherry's voice, "DAVID!"

I have never felt so helpless like this in water! What's wrong with me?

David felt enormous pressure on his chest and lungs and he struggled for breath. Silhouetted figures faded in and out over him through the hazing liquid. *Sherry? Michal?*

He could barely make out some voices. *What did he just say? Did he call me Major?*

"Sir, sir! Can you hear me?

"He's coming to!

"You're going to make it! We're almost there now! You'll be alright!"

Wha, wha...? David couldn't speak. There was something covering his nose and mouth. Ironically, it seemed to be helping him breathe better than before.

Don't try to talk, sir! We are taking good care of you, you're in good hands. The best surgeon in Iraq is waiting for us! We'll touch down in 3 mikes!

Wha, wha...? David wanted to ask him so many questions.

Don't talk sir! Your plane went down. You will make it! You're going to make it!